LADY SCOT

Always a Scot
Book Two

Jade Lee

ARE YOU SIGNED UP FOR DRAGONBLADE'S BLOG?

You'll get the latest news and information on exclusive giveaways, exclusive excerpts, coming releases, sales, free books, cover reveals and more.

Check out our complete list of authors, too!

No spam, no junk. That's a promise!

Sign Up Here

www.dragonbladepublishing.com

Dearest Reader;

Thank you for your support of a small press. At Dragonblade Publishing, we strive to bring you the highest quality Historical Romance from some of the best authors in the business. Without your support, there is no 'us', so we sincerely hope you adore these stories and find some new favorite authors along the way.

Happy Reading!

CEO, Dragonblade Publishing

Additional Dragonblade books by Author Jade Lee

Always a Scot Series
Lord Scot (Book 1)
Lady Scot (Book 2)

Lords of the Masquerade Series
Lord Lucifer (Book 1)
Lord Satyr (Book 2)
Lord Ares (Book 3)

The Lyon's Den Connected World
Into the Lyon's Den
Lyon Hearted

CHAPTER ONE

MacCleal Castle, Scotland

MAIRI SWEATED AS she pulled molten glass into the shape of a swan. It was part of the MacAdaidh crest, for all that she was thought of as a MacCleal now, and she worked hard to fashion a stopper for the perfume bottle she'd made an hour ago.

She made a horrible botch of it.

Disgusted, she threw it into the rubbish bucket. The crash as the glass splintered made her wince. It was the sound of failure, and she was none too pleased with the sensation. Especially since that pit-of-the-stomach knot had been part of her life for a month now, and she was right tired of it.

Her father, the master glassmaker here, looked over at the sound, his brows raised in question. As was their custom, she said nothing. He nodded as if he understood, then went back to blowing another bottle for MacCleal whisky. She would have gone back to work as well if not for another failure walking their way.

Liam MacCleal and his new wife Lady Clara approached, looking grim. Well, Liam looked grim. His wife looked distracted as she worried at her lower lip. She held a letter in her hand and was no doubt figuring some advanced mathematical computation in her head, usually as it pertained to plumbing. They were re-building the old bath house and the lady was instrumental in calculating the waterworks.

The sight of them holding hands stung Mairi's pride. She'd been the one destined to marry Liam—or so she'd been told since birth—and to see him now so happy with his new bride hurt. But no more so than seeing Connall bringing up the rear of the little party.

Connall, the future Duke of Aberbeag, looked like a god on this hot afternoon. He wore little beyond his clan tartan, and his golden hair waved over tawny skin on his very broad chest. She'd known the man since childhood, and he'd smiled like he knew her every secret. Not just hers, but everyone's, and damn it, she was woman enough to see how very appealing he was with his gorgeous muscle and confident smile.

She was also smart enough to know that his presence beside Liam's scowl and Clara's distraction meant no good at all for her. Then he made it worse by laughing at her.

"Lord, Mairi, you'd think someone'd just killed yer pet cat. No need to scowl on such a fine day."

"It's hot as blazes today," she retorted. "And you've not one idea about my cat."

He raised his hand. "Then come on out of that oven there and tell me about yer sweet puss."

She didn't have a cat, and well he knew it. There were cats and dogs aplenty about the MacCleal castle, and she'd cared for many of them. But she was no longer chatelaine, and so there were no animals for her to tend, no tasks for her to complete, and no reason to talk to Connall at all.

She pointedly turned her shoulder to the arrogant man and glared at Liam. "And what's the problem then? One that requires the three of you to give me the news."

"Ach, Mairi," her father said as he set his exquisite glass bottle to cool. Lord, he made it look so easy. "Why must ye always assume the worst?"

Experience? Liam's face? Even his new wife looked worried as she spun the letter over and over in her fingers. She was also the one person who would give Mairi a straight answer, so the next question was directed to her.

"The men seem to be obfuscating today. Lady Clara, can you tell me what's going on?" She was particularly proud of using the word "obfuscate." It meant to hide or obscure, and she'd learned it yesterday from the new teacher, Miss Juliet Adams.

"Lilah's sister is increasing," Lady Clara said. "And she needs more help than expected."

What the bollocks was the woman talking about?

Liam brought his wife's hand up for a gentle kiss. "I think they need more explanation," he said, adoration filling his expression enough to sicken everyone but Lady Clara, who likely didn't even notice.

"What? Oh. That's the London way of saying she's pregnant."

Mairi knew what the word meant. She had no idea why it was relevant. Fortunately, Liam had an explanation.

"I believe Lady Diana intended to sponsor you to London society. She knew her condition before, but still planned to help. Unfortunately, she's a great deal more tired than she expected, and her doctor has declared the strain of a Season too much of a risk."

Oh damnation, hells bells, and every other curse she could think of. She'd lived around men most of her life, so she knew quite a few. She needed a woman to sponsor her to the Marriage Mart or she'd never catch a husband. "But I won't be a strain on her," she said slowly, her gaze hopping back to Lady Clara's. "We're attending parties, not working in a forge. Plus, I know some tonics that can help ease the nausea." She bit her lip. "Is she very delicate?"

"Diana? Goodness, no. She's hale enough that everyone thought she'd murdered her husband."

No response to that except to gape.

"Oh," Lady Clara said when she noticed everyone staring. "She didn't kill him. His son did. But that's not important. She and her new husband Lucas are blissfully happy and now are going to have a family."

"But if she's not delicate, then she can attend a party—"

"Polite society pretends that pregnancy doesn't happen. Babies are given to them by storks. It's a very strange idea."

Clearly. But then the English were a very strange people.

"She meant to buck society, so to speak, but now that her doctor has declared bedrest, she has decided to retire to the country."

Mairi felt her hopes begin to wither inside her. "But then who is to sponsor me?"

"Well, as to that—" Connall began, but she held up her hand.

"You've nothing to do with this," she said tartly. He'd been nothing but a thorn in her side since childhood, and she'd not be listening to his nonsense ever again.

"Actually, he does," Liam responded, his tone matter-of-fact. "He was to escort you to London—"

"At the same time he brought the whisky to London." She already knew that. "We're making the bottles now." She gestured to the neat row of cooling glass.

"But my father and his men drank too much of the stock. You know this. There's more aging up every day, but it's not enough right now. Not to turn a good profit."

She dropped her hands on her hips. "And what do I care about MacCleal whisky?" she snapped. "It's not my name nor my fortune tied to it."

"It's mine," rumbled her father, finally joining the conversation. "What need does he have for a glassblower if he's not got a market for his drink?"

She glared at them all. "It's not *my* fortune," she spat back. "I have my dowry. I have my looks. What I don't have is a man!" Then, when Connall opened his mouth, she spoke quickly over whatever mischief he was about to voice. "A man I *want*," she emphasized.

"Even if he's English?" Connall said, with that ever-present tease in his voice grating on her nerves.

"Even if he's English." Hard not to spit out that last word, but she forced it out. She was a Scotswoman through and through. She never thought she'd consider a Sassenach husband, but necessity required she adapt. "The men are in London now." She looked to Lady Clara. "Surely there is another woman who could sponsor me."

The lady nodded slowly and held out her letter. "Diana's mother, the Dowager Countess of Byrn. She's offered to sponsor you, for a small fee, but I wouldn't do it. Not with her. She's, um, fierce."

"I'm fierce."

"You're Scottish fierce. She's English fierce." Clara shook her head. "She frightens me, and my mother could be so disapproving the vicar steered clear."

How very English to believe that disapproval could sway her from her plans. Her future was at stake. "I'll take her sponsorship with gratitude."

"No, you won't," said Liam. "You've got no one to take you to London. The whisky will require a month."

"A month!"

Lady Clara shook her head. "She can't wait that long. She needs to get new clothing made, she needs dance lessons, she needs—"

"To stay here," her father said. "Plenty of time to go next spring. There'll be whisky to transport, a winter to learn these dances, make frocks, and—"

"It'll be too soon for Diana. You'll have to wait a year for her," said Lady Clara.

"A year! That's much too late for a husband."

Her father laughed. "You think all the men will be gone in twelve months? Will they all drop dead from the ague?"

Good God, were they being this stupid on purpose? She was so furious her words clogged in her throat. Fortunately, Lady Clara explained.

"No, she's right," the lady said. "She's already too old."

"Too old!" her father exclaimed. "She's barely twenty-six."

She was turning twenty-nine early next month, but far be it for her to correct them.

Lady Clara shook her head. "Most debutantes are still teenagers."

"Teenagers!" Connall scoffed. "No wonder the Sassenach have milquetoast bairns. They're being raised by children."

"The Scots marry them off even younger sometimes," inserted Liam.

"But we've got stronger women," Connall shot back. Then he winked at Mairi. "And she's of a fine age to marry."

She glared at the man. He was making fun of her when her future was stake. "No twenty-six year old compares well to a seventeen year old. Not even with cosmetics." Especially when she was really twenty-eight.

Her father wrapped a thick arm around her shoulders. "You're plenty beautiful," he said. "You're smart and strong to boot. Any man would be an idiot not to want you."

Then Liam MacCleal was a damned idiot when he'd selected Lady Clara. And he was even more of a fool because he thought the discussion was ended. "There's naught to be done about it, Mairi. The whisky won't be ready, and Connall's busy enough with the shearing. The spring is a better time for everyone."

Everyone but her.

"I'm a grown woman," she said, her voice dark. "I don't need an escort, least of all him and Sadie." That was the name of his cousin who was meant to come along as chaperone. As if Mairi needed the stern gaze of a chaperone to keep her away from Connall. And anyway, Sadie was younger than she was!

"If you want an English husband, you need to play by English rules," Liam said. "That means you don't go running around on your own." His voice was stern as befitted a future laird. But he was barely a year older than her and so his tone had no effect. "You don't know the Sassenach. To them, it'll be bad enough that you're Scottish. Your free ways make it all worse. They won't work in London like they do here."

"Free? You think I'm free here?" The gall of the man nearly choked her. "I've spent the last ten years ordering the cooking, the cleaning, and the wiping of every damned snot nose and dirty arse in the whole damned castle. And now when I'm done with the lot of you, you tell me I can't leave this miserable plot of sheep dung—"

"Mairi!" her father snapped. "This is your home!"

Was it? She'd thought it was for the last twenty-eight years of her life, but Liam had given that future to Lady Clara. And now there was nothing here for her but to leave. "I'm going," she said firmly.

Lady Clara smiled at her, the expression a little distracted. "I'd feel the same way if I were you. There's no place on earth like London." Her gaze softened. "Liam's promised to take me back in the spring. I'd be a poor sponsor myself. I was never accepted by society, but at least I could show you around the city and keep you away from the dangerous parts."

"That won't help me get a husband."

"No," Clara agreed. "It won't."

Connall stepped forward and tried to lay his hand on her shoulder. She dodged it, of course, but that didn't stop his words. "I'll take you in a month when the whisky's ready and the shearing's done," he said. "Have your dresses made in Edinburgh, and Lady Clara can teach you the dances."

"Oh goodness," the lady murmured. "I'm a terrible dancer."

Mairi sighed. "And what will the Dowager Countess of Byrn think of Scots-made gowns?"

"She'd throw them in the rubbish pile," Lady Clara said. "She's been known to do that with London-made gowns that were not up to her standards. I doubt she'd even look at anything made north of Bedford."

There it was. She needed to leave now to have any hope of finding a noble husband. But as sure as she came to that conclusion, the men apparently decided something else entirely.

"A month won't be too long," her father said, as if he understood anything about female things.

"If you help with the glass blowing," Liam offered, "we might have enough whisky in three weeks."

"And what of Sadie?" Mairi demanded. "She needs to be there as much as I."

"Ach," Connall shrugged. "She's younger than you. Not yet twenty-five. She'll be fine to wait a year and be pleased as punch to go next month."

Her father grunted and picked up the blower pipe to begin another glass jar. "It's settled then. Three weeks if we're lucky, four if we're not."

The other two men nodded in agreement and turned to head out. Lady Clara was the only one to remain behind, frowning in sympathy as she looked at Mairi. "That won't be enough time," she said, her voice resigned. "They don't understand what it takes to launch a girl."

"I need to be there now?" she asked, though she already knew the answer.

"No, Mairi. You needed to be there eight years ago. You're a Scot without a title. How big is your dowry?"

"Plenty big," she said firmly. She had scrimped and saved her coins from the very first day she'd worked at the castle. Plus, she'd sold her perfume bottles at the Edinburgh fair. All that coin had been converted into eight fine copper chains to bring to her marriage bed. It might not be property, but most girls had less. "And I'm the daughter of the MacAdaidh laird. That's title enough." It didn't matter that she and her father were the last MacAdaidh left, she came from a fine bloodline.

"That won't help you in London," the lady said. "Isn't there a Marriage Mart in Edinburgh?"

There wasn't. At least not with any woman who could sponsor her. She'd been promised to Liam on the day she was born. No one—least of all her father—had thought she should cultivate the friendship of a woman in Scottish society. Her only hope was in London with the tenuous connection to a dragon of a countess.

Well, she'd never been one to shy from a challenge.

Mairi quietly folded up Lady Clara's letter and tucked it into her skirt pocket. It had the address of the Dowager Countess of Byrn written on it. Over the years, Mairi had travelled to Edinburgh to sell her perfume bottles. How much harder could it be to take a mail coach down to London? And then easily done to find the Dowager Countess of Byrn. Or so she hoped.

CHAPTER TWO

I N TWENTY-EIGHT YEARS, Mairi had done every job possible in the MacCleal castle home, including stable hand. It was nothing for her to pretend to sleep that night, then gather a very small bag of her belongings, ride to Edinburgh, then board the mail coach first thing in the morning. She paid the innkeeper to return the horse. She'd not have Liam say she stole a horse from him. Then she climbed aboard the top of the coach and fell asleep curled around her bag. She had her full dowry of copper chains in her bag, save the one around her neck, hidden beneath her shift. She would not show herself to be wealthy by flaunting those things. Indeed, she wondered if she should hide them all in her bag.

The weather was drizzly which saved her from the heat but soaked her through. By afternoon, though, the sun came out and baked her in her wet things. And when a man seated next to her tried to take advantage, she kicked him hard enough to make him howl. It took a moment for him to realize that she wasn't trapped up here with him, but he trapped with her. If he encroached on her space, she pinched him with all the strength in hands that had shaped molten glass. And how satisfying it was to take out her ire on a man who deserved it.

The trip to London took nearly two days. When they finally disembarked, she was thoroughly miserable and had a pounding headache. Thankfully, all that was left was to present herself to the dowager countess and pray she appeared better than she felt.

But how to get there? The innyard was a chaotic mass of people. Certainly, she'd seen such busy places in Edinburgh, but she hadn't realized how much the language changed as they went south. She had to concentrate to follow conversation. And she had to enunciate clearly if she wanted to be understood. Given her general exhaustion, that was very hard indeed.

She went inside the inn to ask for directions, but the innkeeper was nowhere to be seen. The main room was bustling, and not a soul wanted to speak to her. She grabbed a barmaid nonetheless. The woman was overworked and none too pleased, but Mairi was determined.

"How do I get here?" she asked, showing the woman the address written in Lady Clara's letter. It was a stupid thing to do. The woman couldn't read. But Mairi was at the end of her rope and her accent was too thick for these people to listen carefully enough to help her.

The boy came out of nowhere. Normally, she would have seen him. Normally she would have held onto her bag. But she was trying to talk to the barmaid when a boy grabbed her small bag and ran straight out the door.

Mairi tried to stop him. Hell, she ran straight out after the child. But the boy was quick as a rat and scurried around a corner long before she could catch him. She ran anyway. Her dowry was in that bag!

She scurried around corners, she dashed down alleys. She ran as if her life depended upon it. And in the end, she failed. Her entire future was gone with her dowry.

And now she was lost in the rats' warren of London streets having chased the damned boy everywhere she could imagine. She stumbled to a stop in the middle of the street, gasping for breath. It was dark here, the gas lamps barely giving any light except in greasy pools. And now she was truly alone in a place where even the burliest of men went carefully.

More than one person looked at her. Even a stray dog licked

his chops as he eyed her.

There was nowhere for her to go. Nothing for her to do except try to find her way back to the inn. Or to someone who could read.

Things got worse instead of better. She could not make sense of the streets and she dared not ask directions of the rough souls who eyed her with greedy eyes.

She quickly became desperate, on the verge of dropping on her knees before man and God to beg for help. She'd been whispering a prayer for fifteen minutes. Thankfully, it was answered before she panicked.

She found the Watch. Two men, one young enough to be barefaced and one with a thick mustache. They whistled as they walked the street and she all but collapsed against them. Thankfully, she'd known enough to look for them, and when she tried to explain what had happened, she become more frustrated still.

"What did ye say?" the mustached man asked. "I can't understand it."

God damn them! Why couldn't they understand simple English?

Because it was Scottish, is why. She took a breath and tried again. Slowly.

"I think she's been robbed," said the younger one. "Look at her. Come from the inn, did you? Down from the mail coach?"

"Yes!" It was the least of the information she wanted to convey, but it was a start.

"Robbed, then?" said the big one. "What'd you lose?"

"Everything!" All she had left was the sodden letter shoved in her pocket.

"Well, that's right hard. Did you get a look at the thief?"

She hadn't. It had happened so fast. "A boy. This tall. Fast."

"Yep," they both said nodding.

"You know him? You can get my bag—"

"You'll never see it again, miss. Not a single thing. There's thousands of them boys in London. Got to hold on to yer things."

She'd set it at her feet while she was talking to the barmaid. She'd used two hands to open up the letter. She couldn't... She didn't...

She began to weep.

She was not a woman who cried, but her whole future was gone. In a single moment, all her scrimping and saving, all the carefully collected coins from a lifetime. All gone.

"Do you have family, miss? Someone who can help you?"

She nodded. She didn't, but she had a name, and it would have to do. "The Dowager Countess of Byrn."

And boy, did that light a fire under them. They straightened up with shock, they fell over themselves to hold her elbow as if she were about to collapse. She wasn't. Well, maybe she was, then they both started talking rapidly. Each spilling over the other to help her.

"You shouldn't be out alone, miss."

"Didn't she send someone to get you?"

"You're in the wrong place, miss. Any number of terrible things might happen."

Something horrible *did* happen! She lost everything!

"Good thing we're here to help."

"Where is her house?"

She told them, enunciating clearly and showing them the letter. Neither of them could read, but she got the information across. Thank God.

"We'll take you right there, miss. We'll need a hackney. Don't suppose you've got any coins to pay do you?"

She had nothing. Everything was gone.

"Don't you worry. I'll bet the countess will pay fer you." His eyes narrowed. "You do know her, don't you? Not lying, are you?"

She frowned at him then held up her proof. Though they couldn't read it, she pointed straight at the words. "Dowager Countess of Byrn."

"Right you are, then. This way, miss."

She followed miserably in their wake. She knew she looked horrendous. She was grateful to finally climb into a hackney. At least that got her out of the dark. The two men kept up a steady noise of conversation. She hadn't the focus to sort through their words, but their patter was comforting enough. Clearly, she needed to work on her accent. It would be impossible to find a husband if he couldn't comprehend a word she said!

But then how was she going to catch a husband at all if she didn't have a dowry? Fear nearly choked her, and she pressed a hand to her chest. Oh goodness! There was her one copper chain. The one she wore down here. Why hadn't she worn all of them? What a fool she'd been!

At least she had the one. That would be something, right? A little bit of money as a pitiful dowry.

The hackney pulled to a stop and the two watchmen helped her descend. They escorted her right up to the front door and pounded the knocker. A sour-faced butler glared down at the three of them.

"Begging your pardon, sir, but this here gel says she belongs to the Dowager Countess of Byrn. Poor thing was robbed and lost in the rookery. She's got nothing now except this letter of recommendation with her. Leastways that's what we think it is. Go on now, gel. Tell 'im."

It took all of her concentration to follow the watchman's flurry of words. It took her even longer to realize they were all staring at her waiting for her to say something.

"Yer name, miss," the younger one promised.

Right. "I'm Mairi, daughter of the MacAdaidh laird. The countess is set to sponsor me for the Season." She held up the letter though it was now smudged and torn.

The butler didn't take it. Indeed, he did nothing more than glare at her as if she were a rat brought to his door by a stray cat. And that roused her anger.

"Lady Clara said so," she said clearly. Then when he wouldn't look at her letter, she folded it up neatly and faced off with the rotten man. "You will let me in now, and you will inform the countess that her charge has arrived. You will do this now or by God…" She choked off her next words. It would not do to threaten to wring the butler's bollocks until he screamed.

"Acts like a toff, don't she?" murmured the young watchman. "If you can sort through the Scottish sounds."

The butler must have thought so too. Enough that he took a step back. She had to walk in beneath his imperious nose.

"And see that the cabbie is paid," she ordered. "And tip these men, please. I fear what might have happened if they had not come to my rescue."

She had no idea if the butler understood her. She didn't want to look back. Instead, she went straight to the parlor. She wanted a moment to breathe alone without all the noise around her. It wasn't just the watchmen, but the sound of people everywhere. Looking out the window, all she saw were buildings barely illuminated by gaslight. She heard dogs in the distance and carriage wheels on the cobblestone. Outside, someone cursed and another chattered. Inside, the watchmen continued talking to the butler. The words were incomprehensible to her, and all the noise made her head pound.

So many people and things everywhere! Even in the parlor there was furniture everywhere in a crowded room all covered with beautiful fabric. A table for tea, two footstools for someone's feet, several lamps, and even a beautiful clock. Glass window of good manufacture in the window covered by silk fabric. This was the parlor of a wealthy woman and she…

She looked like a rat dragged in by a stray cat. And without a significant dowry, she might as well be a rodent.

"Good heavens!" a woman exclaimed.

Mairi spun around. There, standing in the doorway and obviously horrified, stood a lady who had to be the Dowager Countess of Byrn. Mairi attempted a smile. She was sure it failed miserably. She chose instead to curtsey.

"Oh my heavens!" the woman gasped. "Parry! Who is in my parlor?"

The butler crossed over to her. "She appears to be Scottish, my lady."

That was it? That was all he had to say? She'd told him who she was.

"She has a letter," continued the butler.

The woman frowned. "A letter? Where?"

Couldn't anyone speak to her? She was standing right here. Except, of course, they had trouble sorting through her accent. Holding onto her temper as best she could, she pulled out the letter and held it out to the countess. The lady took it between two fingers. And, damn it, the paper looked like a smudged, dirty rag, so she couldn't really blame the woman.

"Oh! Heavens!"

The woman clearly had a limited number of curse words at the ready.

"What happened to her?"

"Robbed, my lady. Found by two watchmen who await you there." He gestured with his right index finger to where the men fidgeted with their caps by the front door. The younger one opened his mouth to speak, but was cut off when the older one shoved an elbow in his ribs.

"I don't need to speak with them," the woman said, her voice curdling with disdain.

"Yes, my lady."

"You, however," she said as she looked at Mairi, "are a different story. Have you nothing to say for yourself?"

Yes, she did, damn it. There was a lot she could say about what she'd been through in the last two days. Worse, she hated the thought that perhaps there was the tiniest possibility that Liam and Connall had been right, and she should not have travelled alone. But that didn't matter now. She was here, and she'd be damned if she let it all go to hell now.

"I am Mairi, daughter of the MacAdaidh laird. My blood is

proper, my face is fair, and my morals are pure. I come to London in search of a husband, and Lady Clara said you would be my sponsor. Was she wrong?"

Stupid to challenge the woman this way, but Mairi was not used to being so dismissed. Plus, pride was her only defense against the miserable way she felt. So when the lady didn't respond, Mairi pushed her luck.

"Do you have nothing to say for yourself?" she demanded.

Far from being offended, the woman's lips curled in an odd sort of smile. Half sneer, half amusement. As if she was unused to expressing humor at all.

"Do you have a dowry?"

"A large one," she lied. It was panic that made her lie. She couldn't be turned away. Not after everything! She couldn't go back to Scotland with yet another failure.

"I thought you were robbed."

"It comes from my laird and will be transferred to an English bank as soon as he can manage."

"Hmm. Does it?"

Mairi nodded then pulled out her copper necklace. That was all she had left of her money. But she had to pay her way somehow, and so she might as well make it clear. "This should be enough to get me started, shouldn't it? For you and for my dresses?"

The woman glided forward, and her eyes narrowed as she inspected the chain. "Take it off."

"Do I stay?" Mairi returned.

"Will you do as I tell you? Sit as I command, dance as I direct, even learn to speak civilized English?"

If the last hour had taught her anything, it was that she was thoroughly lost in London. Not because it was a big city, but because she couldn't communicate with anyone. Not easily. So until she got her feet under her, she would have to listen to the countess.

"What good would it be to have a sponsor, if I ignored your

advice?" she asked. "That would be like paying for an expert then doing the job yourself."

"You swear it? Upon your Scottish honor?"

"I do."

Now the woman truly did smile, and it wasn't altogether pleasant. "I expect you're going to hate yourself for that. But even so, I expect you to stick to your word."

"I am not a woman who lies." Except about the size of her dowry.

"We'll see," the woman said, her tone ominous. "Because if I found out you have, then you will be out on your dirty Scottish arse. Do I make myself clear?"

Oh. The woman did have a better cursing vocabulary.

"Yes, my lady."

"Good." She stripped out of her gloves. "Parry, pay the Watchmen—"

"And the cabbie!" cried the younger man.

"—Then get a bath started. First thing is to find out what's underneath all that dirt." She looked at Mairi. "Are you a Scottish rose or a thorn?"

"A thorn, my lady, but I can pretend."

There was a moment of stunned silence in the room, then quite suddenly, the Dowager Countess of Byrn laughed.

All in all, Mairi thought, a good start.

A few hours later, she did indeed regret promising this witch of a woman any damned thing.

CHAPTER THREE

London

C ONNALL HATED TRAVELLING by mail coach. He preferred to control his own destiny, and that included his means of travel. But he could not ride his own cattle all the way to London. At least not at the speed the Sassenach mail coach did. And so he grabbed a seat up top—the only place left—and cursed Miss Mairi MacAdaidh all the way down to London.

He shouldn't have been surprised that she took off the way she had. The woman had a Scot's temper, but it was usually tempered by good sense. Dangerous enough to travel by oneself as a man. To do so as a woman into a city as strange as London? Well, that was reckless on a whole new level.

But he knew that's where she was even before her father confirmed it. From the moment Liam had told him that Mairi had disappeared, he was sure she'd headed down to that harridan of a countess and to hell with any Scotsman who wanted her hand.

Damned bold she was, and he had little choice but to follow. It was the only way he could be sure she was still alive.

He'd taken the fastest route down to London—in the rain, no less—drenched to the bone on top of the mail coach. He knew his way about London, at least enough to get him to her address, but he appeared on the countess's doorstep like a half-drowned rat. And now he stood with his hat in hand, praying that Mairi had made it here safe and sound. And if she was, well, then he planned to throttle her.

The door was opened by a dour-faced butler who curled his lip in disdain. Supercilious Sassenach. There was nothing wrong with crushed clothing if one had just travelled across the country without so much as time for a shave.

"I'm here to see Miss Mairi MacAdaidh," he declared.

"Oh look. Another Scot," the man drawled.

Connall was about to say something biting when he realized the man had said *another* Scot. "She's here then? Safe?"

"And who might you be?" the butler returned, refusing to answer.

"I'm the man charged with seeing to her safety, damn you. Is she here?"

"Then you've done a poor job of it, haven't you? Now who are you?"

"I don't need you to tell me my business," he snapped. "Is she hurt?"

Far from answering, the man drew up to his full height which, for a Sassenach, was plenty tall. And given that he stood a step above Connall, he thoroughly blocked the door. "Your name, sir."

Connall took a breath to blast the man, but then he heard a distinctive voice, thick with brogue and using words best reserved for Scotsmen in the drink.

"Damn yer bluidy book! And damn these infernal boots!" There were more words, softly murmured by someone else, quickly lost amid a flurry of curses that made Connall grin. Only one Scotswoman swore like that, and if she had enough breath to speak loud enough for this butler's ears to turn red, then she was alive and well.

He blew out a relieved breath. "Ye can inform the crabbit lass that Connall Aberbeag, son of the Duke of Aberbeag is here to ring her bonny neck." He'd let his brogue run thick just to confuse the butler. The man would hear the words Duke of

Aberbeag and not make much else out. And that very confusion allowed him to bully his way inside. "Don' mind me," he said. "I'll find her meself."

Fortunately, he was a big man, otherwise he'd never have managed it. When he stepped into the doorway, the butler had to retreat or be bowled over in an undignified heap. And once the man had given up that small bit of space, Connall wasted no time in pushing past to head straight to the parlor where he'd heard Mairi curse.

He hauled the parlor door open. Trust Mairi to curse loud enough to be heard through a closed door. Then he drank in the sight of Mairi with a book on her head looking like a miserable, bright yellow sack of potatoes.

The woman he knew was muscular with strong hands, a willowy waist, and breasts that made a man enjoy the looking. What he saw now was bright yellow fabric with two flounces that hung on her body in misshapen lumps. The scowl on her face was familiar enough to be attractive to him. The way one always smiles at an old friend. But the tilt to her head was new. It made her appear to be staring down her nose at him. He knew the books atop her head caused the new position, and right hilarious she looked balancing them that way.

"Say one word, Connall, and I'll…blast!"

Apparently, the woman couldn't curse at him and keep the books on her head. They tumbled down around her like heavy rain. Thank goodness she wore sturdy half boots, otherwise her toes would have been pummeled.

With the books at her feet, he got a good look at the way her hair was twisted and pinned. Well, no wonder she'd had to tilt her head to an unnatural angle. And he'd bet anything she had a headache from the octopus-like coils of locks.

"Have none of the Scots any manners?" inquired a very English woman who sat ramrod straight on the settee. Obviously, the Countess. Now that he had seen that Mairi was safe—if miserable—then he could make his bows to the lady.

Crossing to the Countess, he took her hand to bow deeply over it. And when he straightened, he spoke as clearly as he could with no trace of Scots in his voice.

"Forgive my intrusion, my lady. I'm afraid Miss MacAdaidh's father was in a panic at her absence yesterday morning and dispatched me to retrieve her. We are all most grateful for you to have given her aid and comfort in her time of need."

He nearly choked on the word "comfort." Mairi looked anything but comfortable, but that wasn't the point. She'd risked a great deal to come here on her own, and he was still furious with her for the danger she'd put herself in.

Typically, Mairi wasn't silent. "My father knew exactly what I'd done. I left a note—"

He rounded on her and let some of his fury boil through. "That's why he was terrified. God's bollocks, Mairi, do you ken what might have happened to ye?" His brogue was thick this time not because he didn't want the English to understand but because he was that furious. "I spent the last two days thinking about what might have happened to ye."

"You've no cause to be thinking about me at all, Connall Aberbeag."

"That's not stopped me one whit from doing it these years and more."

She glared at him, emotions clearly boiling up within her. He watched as her fists raised, ready to strike him, but she held them back. Mad as she was, she knew better than to strike him. Last time she'd tried, he'd… Well, that's what put them in this current state of odds, now, wasn't it?

And then his gaze chanced to land on her hands. Her knuckles were white for the most part as she gripped her fists, but he saw the scrape on them, too. The kind one gets from a fight.

He grabbed her hands, pulling them up to the sunlight to see better. She didn't fight him, probably because he'd startled her. And when she whipped them back down, he let her go. But his tone was deadly serious when he spoke.

"What happened, Mairi? Who'd you fight?"

"It's nothing but a scrape. I got much worse from glass nearly every time."

That wasn't true, and that wasn't the point. "Whom did you fight?"

"You've no cause to be asking me that," she snapped. "I'll give account to my father and no one else."

"And I am here on account of your father. Mairi, who did yo—"

"She was robbed, you idiot Scot," the countess said in a weary voice.

"Robbed!" His gaze leaped to the countess who appeared in earnest. And when he looked back at Mairi, her irritation was plain.

"I didn't scrape my knuckles then," she snapped. She held up her abraded knuckles. "This was from teaching a man on the coach how a proper gentleman treats a lady."

The countess gasped. "Sweat heaven!"

"You were accosted! On the mail coach. And robbed?" Panic shot through him. "Are you hurt? What happened? Mairi—"

"Ach! Quiet yerself!"

He grabbed her arms and looked her in the eyes. "You must tell me it all," he commanded.

Then contrary woman that she was, she simply arched a brow. "And why would I do that? What right have you to demand—"

"Mairi!"

"That's Miss MacAdaidh to you!"

He bit off his angry retort. She was correct. He had no right to demand anything of her, but damn her, he ought to! He wanted to! He had yearned for her since he'd first seen her punch an older boy who was hurting a lamb. She'd been six. She had fire then and now, a fierceness he wanted by his side as they carved out a life in the highlands.

But he'd been a boy and misplayed his hand. And she...

"What did I do to have you treat me so?" he asked. "I've stood with you against the MacCleal when his men got out of hand, I rushed for two days to London to be sure you were safe. I have responsibilities, as well you know, and yet I left without a second thought just to find you."

She sighed as she set her hands on her hips. "Connall Aberbeag, what does a woman have to say to get through your thick head? I am here to find an English husband—"

"And are you that ashamed of your kin? You'll hate the Sassenach here. Not a one could best you in a fight."

"And that's the measure of a man?" she scoffed. Then she punched him right hard in the gut. He'd seen the punch coming and let himself tense for the blow, but he didn't flinch for all that she could hit like a bull. "There now," she said. "You can take a hit better than any English. Is that the only measure of a man? Should I marry ye because you've got a stomach harder than a rock?"

She absently rubbed at her knuckles as her gaze canted away. He surrounded her fist in his own hand, cradling it to show that he could be gentle as well.

"Mairi," he said, keeping his tone chiding. "I don't mean fighting with fists. Ye like a good fight with words, ye like measuring yourself against a man, and there's not an Englishman here who'll know what to do with ye."

"And you do?" she challenged as she tried to pull her hand free.

He didn't let her go. "Aye, I do."

He held her gaze and willed her to soften. He had experienced it once before and the moment was imprinted on his memory like a carving into granite. That time, ten years ago, her jaw had loosened first. A slight softening that flowed up to her eyes. Her shoulders had rolled down as her hands had trembled with conflicting signals. She'd made neither a fist nor fully opened her hands, but had hovered somewhere halfway between. Her body, too, had leaned in and pulled back without any of her customary decisiveness.

Ten years ago, he'd been an idiot. He'd stolen the decision from her and had taken control of her. He'd used his size and his strength, and she'd never forgiven him his enthusiasm. It wasn't just that he'd moved too fast. He had taken the decision away from her, and that was something that Mairi never forgave.

So here he was now, praying that the moment was returning to him. Her jaw softened as her eyes widened. Her body might have swayed, though it was hard to tell. She opened her mouth, probably to say something, but his mind conjured up erotic images in a rapid surge of hunger.

This time, he knew better than to take the invitation. Indecision was not consent, and so he held himself back. Though, naturally, one part of his anatomy strained forward anyway. And while his hands tightened around hers—*please, please, say yes*— panic burst across her expression.

Fear quickly chased away by fury had her eyes flashing and her jaw firming. She took a hard step back from him and nearly toppled a small table in her haste. And that, naturally, made her even angrier.

"I'm fine, Connall Aberbeag without your huge hands all over me. I'll answer to my father and no one else!"

He'd hardly had his hands all over her, but he didn't argue with her. He knew she was referring to that time a decade ago when he'd been a complete ass. Instead, he put his hands in his pocket, wishing he could alleviate some of the pressure down there, and looked at her with frustration.

"The English won't know what to do with ye," he said softly.

"Nevertheless, I mean to try," she countered.

"Oh they'll know," inserted the countess. Connall jolted. He'd forgotten the woman was there. That's how absorbed he got in Mairi's presence. "They'll insult you to your face, call you names that you can overhear, and cut you down in the hopes that some gentleman will look their way. But that's just the women. The men will take your lack of refinement as an excuse. You'll need to keep those fists handy, Miss MacAdaidh."

Furious because he knew it was true, he rounded on the countess. "What good are you to her if you can't keep the gossip away? If she's here and paying you a pretty penny for her chance, you're supposed to present her to respectable gentlemen and not vipers or cads."

The countess stiffened where she sat. "You'll mind your tongue, sirrah."

"Sirrah? You're the one being hired, not me."

He saw the blow hit the lady. She was a countess, and if not a leading lady in society, at least one of its rarer flowers. And yet here she was, reduced to taking money to sponsor a girl into society. And then, showing that she and Mairi were well suited, the lady straightened up to her full height. It was only about three-quarters of his height, and yet she made him feel like a ten-year-old boy before her.

"I was asked by my daughter to sponsor a girl in need." She turned to Mairi. "Are you in need of my help?"

Mairi's response was immediate as she dipped into a graceful curtsey. "Yes, countess. Please."

The lady turned to Connall. "Then what relationship do you have with her that makes this your business? Are you her father or brother? A cousin, perhaps, or her guardian?"

"I am not, my lady." It was the God's honest truth. "But I care for—"

She held up her hand to cut him off. "Then your interest in my relationship with Miss MacAdaidh is impertinent."

He swallowed. She was right, much though that galled him. But he still had an ace up his sleeve. He smiled apologetically at the lady, then lifted his hands as if things were out of his hands. Which they weren't...yet. "My understanding was that you had agreed to sponsor two ladies, yes? Miss MacAdaidh and my cousin Sadie. They were meant to travel here together, in private conveyance, with my escort."

The countess frowned. "Yes, that was my understanding."

"Well, as I am responsible for my cousin's debts, I believe your arrangement is with me."

"When you present this cousin, I will, of course, discuss such things with you." She arched a brow at Mairi. "And if she is anything like Miss MacAdaidh, then I suggest you get her here immediately. There is much work to do, and they might as well learn their lessons together."

Mairi snorted. "Unless you plan to make her wait another year." She glanced at the Countess. "Sadie is younger than me by a few years."

The lady shuddered. "That is still too old. She cannot wait." That last had the force of a command.

Connall ground his teeth. "There are other considerations. I still have the shearing to do, and she's still in mourning for her Ma who passed some months ago."

Both women scoffed at him. "A man's excuse," said the countess.

"He likes his women dependent upon his good nature," Mairi said. "He does not want us to marry."

That was not true, and so he had said. But neither one listened.

The countess folded her arms. "Is this Sadie as independent as you?"

"Yes," Mairi affirmed.

God help him, she was right.

"Will she come on her own? If we know the time, we can meet her at the innyard. Though I shudder to think—"

"Absolutely not! She will not travel here alone!" Good God, the idea that any woman he knew would be subjected to unwanted attention made his blood run hot. But the moment the words were out of his mouth, he knew he'd walked straight into a trap.

"I'm glad you agree," said the countess with a smile. "You are quite correct, of course. It's most dangerous on the mail coach and if word got out…" She shuddered. "Well, it would severely handicap her ability to wed. I'm so glad you will bring her down without delay. Hopefully, she will learn to speak proper English as quickly as Miss MacAdaidh. Indeed, I can almost understand her now."

"Thank you, countess," Mairi said with a sweet smile. Then both women turned to him as if he had agreed to this mad plan.

"I cannot bring Sadie here this week. Not after losing it to Mairi."

"You do not wish to see your cousin happy?" the countess asked.

"You are being unreasonable."

The countess folded her arms. "Mr. Aberbeag, you keep speaking of your responsibilities. You are the son of the laird, yes? The duke's eldest son?"

"Yes."

"Then you also have responsibilities to the women of your clan. Your cousin is well past an age to marry. You have hurt her chances enormously by waiting this long. And you will hurt her even further if she does not get the training she requires immediately. To honor your *duty* to her, you must bring her here. Immediately."

There was no quarter in her words or expression, and truth be told, he'd felt the weight of that neglect more of late. Perhaps from the moment Sadie had reminded him of it and demanded her Season in London.

"I do not understand what is wrong with Scotsmen!"

The countess threw up her hands. "Well, neither do I! English gentlemen know when and how to present their daughters or they know how to listen to their wives about such things. I can only assume that your father is a widower. Sad that he had no wife to explain such things to him."

That was not at all what he meant. He wondered why Mairi and Sadie couldn't marry at home when there were several good men interested. But he was outmatched here and not because the countess said so, but because Mairi and Sadie were old enough to know their own minds. And clearly, they both wanted a Sassenach.

28

Or they would think that until they got a good look at the milquetoast offerings in London. Telling him they were wrong would do no good at all. They had to learn that for themselves.

He knew it was the truth, but damn it, it was still hard to leave Mairi to see it in her own time.

"I could make you happy," he said softly to Mairi.

She shook her head. "I make my own happiness, Connall." She gave him a wistful smile. "Mayhap you should stay here. Many a lass will want a future duke for all that she'd have to live in Scotland."

True. But he wanted no other. Meanwhile, the countess leaped upon that idea.

"Excellent!" she cried. "Find gentleman's quarters nearby. You shall be our escort once the Season begins in earnest. It's only the Little Season, of course, but having a future duke at our side will increase everyone's consequence."

Especially the countess's, but he wouldn't argue, especially as it kept him near Mairi's side. He had one last question, though, before he committed to this bizarre time in London when he and his people were busiest.

"Mairi, you still haven't answered my question about the robbery. Are you all right? How much did you lose?"

"Nothing of import, Connall Aberbeag. And that's all you need to know."

She was lying. He could see it in her eyes. The robbery had shaken her, but he had no right to help her if she refused his aid. So he did the only thing he could. He turned to the countess. "I will be your escort this Season. See that the ladies are exposed to gentlemen of quality."

"Naturally!" the woman sounded insulted that he could think otherwise.

And after the women saw that even the best Englishman couldn't measure up to a good Scotsman, they would both return fully chastened and ready to find a real man in the country of their birth.

CHAPTER FOUR

MAIRI'S SHOULDERS AND neck hurt bad enough to give her a pounding headache. It was the result of keeping her head held rigid all damned day while a book kept sliding off her ridiculous haircut. Did English women really do this? No wonder they were so often in foul moods. Today's experience was enough to make Mairi sour on the whole world.

Thankfully the day was done. The sun was down, dinner consumed, and the countess had retreated to her bedroom to "soothe her frazzled spirit." Mairi wanted a spirit of a different sort. Some good Scot's whisky would do her good, but there was none of that here, and she had no idea if the lady would approve of drinking or not. So instead, Mairi lay on her bed with her arm over her eyes and hoped that the pounding would end.

It didn't. In fact, it was echoed by a knock on her door. Mairi was still deciding if she would pretend she'd died when the door opened and the countess swept in.

"Oh, don't be such a pout. Sit up. We could both use some of this, I think."

Mairi let her arm drop to see the lady holding out a glass of a dark liquid. Her nose twitched and her brows rose. "What is that?"

"French brandy. It's not often that I open a new bottle, but I'm celebrating today. Not one, but two ladies to bring out." She smiled as she handed over a glass. "When Lilah married, I thought I'd never have a companion again. But now I've got two new ladies to bring out. Two!" she said gleefully as she sipped from her glass. "You can split the duties between you, but for now, I'm afraid it will all fall upon you. But never mind that now. I've got something else to discuss with you."

Mairi straightened up on the bed. "Duties? What duties?"

"The running of a household, of course. You've got to learn that before any man will marry you."

"I've been running a castle for nearly ten years. I think I can manage an Englishman's household."

"We'll have to see about that, won't we? We'll have an evening soiree before the Season opens. A small affair of twelve. I've selected the date and you'll discuss the meal plans with Cook tomorrow morning before your fitting. If you're organized, it shall be a breeze."

Mairi was organized, but dinner for a dozen in an English house likely meant all sorts of customs to be learned. Though she'd routinely fed several dozen, she'd done it at a castle where the meat came out on platters, the bread was often thrown at the guests, and the drink was managed (or mismanaged) by the laird.

"Don't frown at me. I'll teach you everything you need to know. That's why you're paying me." Her expression sobered as she waved at Mairi. "Drink up! Drink up! We've got to discuss something delicate and it's easier to do such things with drink." She shrugged. "I never had to have these discussions before Lilah married. She handled the unpleasantness. But I've had to learn with all my daughters gone and my son finally starting his nursery."

Her expression took up a tragic air as if having four children married well was a terrible burden. It wasn't, but Mairi had quickly learned that the countess had her own way of looking at things.

"Drink!"

Mairi jolted at the sudden command and rapidly took a big gulp. It was too much, too fast and she choked on it. But she was used to whisky, so she recovered quickly enough. And then she set the mostly full glass beside the bed.

"What did you want to discuss, my lady?"

The woman frowned at Mairi's nearly full glass. "I have launched three daughters to brilliant matches. Gwen was a disaster, of course, but I finally showed her the way. Diana was angry at me, but she's blissfully happy now. And Lilah, well you know the problem there. My husband's by-blow, married to an earl!"

From what Mairi had heard, none of those matches were thanks to the countess, but she knew better than to argue.

"My girls and I had our problems. Gwen wouldn't listen to a word I said about anything, but there was one thing that kept us going. One thing that allowed for brilliant matches. Do you know what that was?"

"No, my lady. What?"

"They never lied to me. Not once. They said awful things to me, things that I didn't like. But I'd rather that than a lie. I can't help you if you're dishonest."

Mairi swallowed. The countess's expression was firm, but there was sympathy in her eyes. And Mairi felt her lies come up and choke her.

"I'm going to ask you some questions, Mairi, and mind that I will know if you lie. I'm not as stupid as some might think. Swear you will answer honestly. Swear on your mother's soul."

Oh my. The woman was laying it on thick, but it was working. She would not lie on her dead mother's soul. She couldn't.

"First question, are you a virgin?"

Mairi jolted. "What?"

"Something has happened between you and the duke. Something that—"

"He's not a duke yet!" Mairi snapped.

"But have you already given yourself to him?"

"No! I've not lain with a man ever!" Mairi's face was hot, and her hands clenched.

"And a doctor would verify such a thing?"

Mairi recoiled. "They can do that?"

"Some claim so. We can find one to bribe if need be—"

"No! I have never been with a man." She all but shouted the words.

The countess took a deep breath and released it, satisfaction in her expression. "Good. Now how much—exactly—is your dowry?"

There was nothing she could say to that. Not a single word. It had been hard enough to defend her virginity, but this... She looked down at her hands.

"It's all gone, isn't it?" the countess asked. "It was in your bag?"

Mairi nodded miserably. "I had enough. I had a good dowry, but—"

"Yes, yes. At least you managed to save that one necklace. I've already had it converted in my account. It will pay for dresses and my fee, but it won't go any further than that."

The words were like knives in her heart. What was she going to do?

"Don't worry. That's enough to get us started this Season, but you'll have to make some serious decisions right now."

"What kind of decisions?"

"You can't marry for love. It will need to be for money. There are several gentlemen possessed of an acceptable fortune who want a young bride. Widowers, mostly, or men who..." Her voice trailed away as she finished off the rest of her brandy. "They've got unusual appetites. If you are amenable to—"

"No. Absolutely not."

The lady narrowed her eyes. "Virgins don't usually know what I'm referring to."

"I've been chatelaine to the MacCleal clan for nearly a decade. That means I controlled the laird's men by being meaner and faster than any of them. I know about men's appetites."

"Do you? Truly?"

Mairi blushed. "I know about some of them, and I've heard whispers about others."

"Your father should have protected you better."

"My father kept me from being one of their appetites."

The woman pursed her lips. "Is that who taught you to punch?"

No, that had been Connall. He knew that the men were interested in her before anyone else, and he taught her to defend herself from everyone but him.

"It wasn't your father?" the lady pressed.

"I learned some from him, some from others." Mairi took refuge in her brandy rather than say more.

"Hmmm," the lady said as she watched Mairi drink. "Well, I suppose it's enough that you did learn. Now tell me why you won't marry a duke."

She should have expected that question. After all, everyone back home thought she was daft for not choosing the future Aberbeag laird. It mattered less in Scotland that he was a duke, but it still mattered. And the countess probably thought she was completely daft for showing Connall the door.

"Is he poor?"

Mairi shook his head.

"Deviant?"

She gasped in horror. "Of course not!"

The countess's expression implied that nothing in this world was a matter "of course," but she didn't argue. "Did he hurt you, then? Or do you imagine that you will fall desperately in love with an Englishman?"

That wasn't what she thought. Well, not exactly. "Liam fell in love with an Englishwoman." And when the countess didn't understand, she quickly explained. "Lord Loughton married Lady Clara in Scotland. And they—"

"Oh yes. Lilah's odd bird of a friend. So she made a match of it then? And they are in love?"

"Apparently," Mairi groused as she drank more brandy. "I

was to be his bride. His father and my father agreed on the day I was born, and so I became chatelaine."

"But the gentleman didn't want you?"

Mairi winced and took refuge in her drink.

"And now you're here because you're sulking? Because you've been rejected—"

"No!" How could she explain something she barely understood herself? "I have known the men of the MacCleal clan all my life. And Connall's clan is no less familiar."

"Are they all as handsome as him?"

"No. That's Connall's great pride. He's got a pretty face and a bonnie body." That was putting it mildly. There was no equal in face and form to Connall Aberbeag, and he knew it.

"A vain man, then. It's a hard path to marry a man who is prettier than oneself. I don't blame you one bit."

Connall was more than a pretty face, and she took issue with the thought that the man was prettier than her. But she wasn't given a chance to object as the countess continued on.

"Marriage must be looked at in a practical way. Without a dowry, he's the best you're likely to get. And that's assuming he wants you as a wife and not a mistress."

"I'd twist his bollocks right off if—"

"That's enough of that!" The words were sharp as Mairi quieted immediately. The lady waved a hand in front of her red face, clearly overcome by heat whether from embarrassment or drink. The lady moderated her tone. "I'll steer you to gentlemen who won't mind that you're penniless. If love blooms, then everyone's happy. But if it doesn't, you'll need to take my direction and marry the man best suited to your situation. Do you understand me?"

She did not. "Exactly what kind of man is best suited to me?"

"A Scotsman, I should think—"

"No!"

"Then a widower or cit. We'll see. Magic can happen if you prepare for it." She narrowed her eyes. "And you will be preparing a great deal in the next few weeks. Best resign yourself to it."

"I've worked hard all my life," began Mairi, but the lady waved her hands furiously in front of Mairi's face.

"Oh, for heaven's sake, don't ever mention that!"

Mairi bit her lip. Just how much of herself would she have to hide?

Meanwhile, the countess leaned back in her chair. "Now that that's settled, it's time to discuss your dresses. And your hair. And your accent." The lady folded her arms across her chest. "They all have to change."

CHAPTER FIVE

Aberbeag Castle, Scotland

I T WAS WELL before dawn when Iseabail Spalding banged on her dearest friend's door. Her friendship with Sadie Allen of the clan Aberbeag was tenuous at best, but Iseabail held their whispered conversations close. All seven of them. Six had been brief exchanges, the last being a shared look across booths at the summer festival, but the first had created a friendship that she prayed would stand strong now.

Seven years ago, they had both escaped their keepers to wander blissfully free. Sadie's mother had been happier then and had given her daughter a few hours to explore. Iseabail's mother had been alive, and she'd watched the two girls from afar as they became fast friends.

Seven years ago.

Tonight, Iseabail's life depended upon a girl she'd spent no more than four hours with so long ago.

Taking her faith in her hands, she banged hard on the door again. Where was Sadie? Had she moved? No, she couldn't have. This was the cabin. She'd found that out specifically. Unless it had been a lie. Then what would she do? She hadn't eaten in two days, and she hadn't slept in longer. Sadie was her last hope.

A light sparked within the small crofter hut. Thank the lord!

"Sadie! Sadie, please…"

The door hauled open, and a dour faced man scowled at her. "Wot you doing, woman?"

She thought about running, but she'd already run so far. And where would she go? "I'm looking for Sadie Allen. She lived here with her mother."

"Her ma died. Months ago. She's up at the castle now. Taking off to London with Connall."

London? With the future laird? "When?" she whispered.

"Today. Tomorrow. Yesterday." He shrugged as if it weren't a matter of life and death to her.

"Yesterday?" Panic choked off her breath.

"Why are you waking a man..."

Iseabail didn't wait to hear more. She had a rough idea where the Aberbeag castle was, and terror lent wings to her feet. If Sadie had gone to London yesterday, then Iseabail was doomed for sure.

She made it to the back of the castle by morning, stumbling forward and begging everyone to find Sadie for her. Someone pulled Iseabail into the kitchen where she sank to her knees, her strength completely gone.

"Iseabail? Is that you?"

She looked up, her eyes wide at the familiar voice.

"Iseabail—"

"No! I'm not... I'm..." Her words failed her. She didn't want anyone here to know her real name. Fortunately, Sadie understood. She waved the men in the kitchen away. Iseabail watched with grateful eyes as the rough Aberbeag men left the kitchen with barely a backward glance. The constriction in her chest eased with every step they took away from her. Meanwhile, Sadie looked at the girl who slept near the fire.

"Can you scoop up some stew, Chloe?" she asked. "My friend and I will sit here and eat a bit, then we'll run up to my chamber while everyone else goes back to sleep."

Iseabail's eyes welled up with gratitude. Sadie was as fierce as she remembered, able to take control when Iseabail had always been more timid. Well, she hadn't been timid today, but she was out of her depth now and exhausted. And hungry.

The food was delicious. At this point, a rotten apple would likely taste delicious to her, but this was wholesome mutton stew. She gulped it down like a starving dog while Sadie watched with a slightly startled expression. She didn't argue though or ask questions Iseabail couldn't answer. She simply waited in silence after she shooed Chloe to bed.

Eventually, Iseabail ate her full. In time, her belly bulged, and her eyes began to droop. Sadie gently guided her up to a bedchamber at the top of the castle. It wasn't fancy and it wasn't large, but it was warm and had a bed. Iseabail would have collapsed into it if she had a right to. But she didn't. She needed to explain exactly what had happened and what she needed from a girl she hadn't spoken to in years.

Sadie spoke first. "Tell me what happened. Is it your uncle?"

Her uncle was Baron Bain, the head of her clan and her guardian. Iseabail didn't even think he was a real baron but had simply adopted the title when he became laird after his brother's death. The man was a mean drunk, a vicious warrior, and had terrorized her and her mother since the day her father died and her uncle started leading.

"My uncle wants to marry me to one of his men." Iseabail said with a shudder. "Albie's old, smells, and killed his own dog out of meanness. The women won't go near him, and my uncle plans to marry me to him." Fear choked off her words.

"Is it for your dowry?"

She nodded. "I told my uncle I'd give it to him if he set me free, but he wouldn't take it."

Sadie tilted her head in confusion. "Why not? I thought that's what he wanted."

Iseabail did, too, but she'd long since given up trying to understand the man. "He says it would be dishonorable." What he probably meant was that it would appear dishonorable, and he couldn't do that. He had no difficulty murdering people in their sleep so long as no one knew it was him who had killed her father. But Iseabail knew. As had her mother.

Sadie pulled her down to sit on the bed. "How did you escape?"

"I drugged the men with the laudanum they've been giving me. Then I ran."

"All the way here? But that's miles!"

What could she say to that? It was true. She'd done it because she was desperate. "I have to hide, Sadie. If he finds me, he'll kill me. Or marry me to that monster." She grasped her friend's hands. "I'll do anything. I'll scrub the floors, I'll slop the pigs. You have to hide me."

Sadie shook her head. "He'll find you here. We sell him copper, and too many people already saw you arrive."

Iseabail felt the walls close in on her. What would she do if Sadie couldn't help? There were no other options. Even her mad dash across Scotland had been an act of insane desperation. Her mind spun into darkness, and she had no strength to speak or cry or even stop the descent. All she knew was fear beating inside her until she heard Sadie cry her name.

"Iseabail! Iseabail, listen. I have an idea."

Did she? That was good because Iseabail had nothing left.

"Connall's taking me to London. You remember my cousin? I'm to have my Season there. We're leaving as soon as the shearing's done."

"London?" That was far away. Maybe far enough that her uncle couldn't find her.

"Yes." Sadie smiled, and the expression softened the care lines around her face. "I'm to find a husband."

"In London? Why go there?"

"Why not there? My blood is good enough, my dowry, too. There's no one here who I want so—"

"Take me with you," Iseabail begged. "I'll be your maid. My uncle won't find me there. I can be free." The word *free* echoed in her head. Anything was better than what her life had been there.

"I don't know if I can," Sadie said, biting her lip. "My cousin thinks it's just me."

Iseabail gripped her mother's necklace, the only proof she had of her identity. It was a dragon in the vague shape of a shield, and it said to those who believed the old tales that her heart beat for Scotland as a woman descended of many women, all bound to the land. According to her mother, with the necklace came a dowry of five hundred gold coins to be handed to Iseabail's husband. Truthfully, she doubted that a single coin was left. Her uncle had probably spent them all, but he liked to pretend he was a man of honor. And so the story of her dowry was well known as was her title. In English circles, she was the Honorable Miss Spalding, granddaughter of the Earl of Spalding and ward of Baron Bain.

"Please, Sadie," she begged. "I will do anything. Just hide me away."

"Hiding you won't be enough," her friend said. Then she gestured to the pillows behind her. "Right now, you need sleep. We'll face what's to be done in the morning."

"But—"

"Hush. Neither of us can think right now."

Iseabail didn't need much more urging. Her eyes were half-closed as it was. She nearly crawled to the bed, shedding her filthy clothes as she went. Moments later she was asleep.

Two days later, she was dressed as a maid, wrapped in a thick blanket, and headed to London.

CHAPTER SIX

Aberbeag Castle, Scotland

C ONNALL WAS NOT a fool. He knew that his cousin's new maid was not normal. Certainly, they both knew every titled lady had her own maid, but Sadie had lived without servants for the last five years of her mother's life. That wasn't lack of money but because Sadie's mother had been a viper-tongued shrew, and no servant stuck around for that kind of abuse. The Scots were a sturdy lot, but some things were too much for even them.

So Sadie's sudden maid had to be something else.

"Who is she?" he demanded as they loaded up the carriage.

"My maid," was the only answer.

And since he'd been awake the night through shearing sheep, he hadn't the strength to argue. The woman seemed meek enough and vaguely familiar. Nothing in her appearance or his memory told him to beware. And Sadie generally had a good head on her shoulders. So he shot his cousin a hard look as she put one foot in the carriage.

"I'll know the answer before we make London," he said firmly.

"Connall, please—" She cut off her words as he tugged her backwards hard enough that she stumbled back onto the ground.

"Swear, Sadie, or I'll not take either of you."

His cousin bit her lip then nodded.

"Sadie—"

"I swear!" she cried. "Now can we please go?"

"We can," he agreed. He let her climb back into the carriage and was much too grateful when he was at last able to sit down. Shearing sheep was an exhausting activity, hard for most men to do for a day. He'd been at it all week and through the night. It was finished, thank God, but he was bone tired. He planned to sleep at least until Edinburgh if not halfway to London.

He didn't count on getting a fever.

It wasn't surprising, given how hard he'd worked to get the shearing done. Every part of his body ached from the work or so he'd thought. It was a fever, and now he was shivering in the carriage and cursing every damned bump in the road.

If he were alone, he'd hole up in an inn until the worst of it passed. Indeed, the women suggested it, but he had a schedule to keep. He knew that there was a dangerous stretch of road in northern England, one renowned for highwaymen. Aaron had recommended a group of men who protected travelers. Their leader was Reuben Bates, and the man had agreed to meet Connall's carriage in Halifax and escort it the rest of the way to London.

Unfortunately, they were already a day late. He didn't want to make Reuben wait any longer just to huddle in a bed and feel miserable. Better to huddle in the carriage and feel miserable and at least make progress toward London.

So that's what they did while he shivered beneath blankets and the carriage made its way toward Halifax. The women whispered to each other, sharing quiet secrets while they cast worried eyes in his direction. If he felt better, he'd tease the truth out of them with charm. As it was, he wrapped himself in depressing thoughts about his father who was dying and the woman he'd longed for since he was a boy.

He'd left Mairi in London to suffer the countess's "gentle" instruction. He'd rushed back home to finish the shearing and escort Sadie to London. But during every moment of the last week, he'd thought about Mairi.

No other woman matched him in sass, fists, or sheer stubborn blindness. As children, they'd traded verbal barbs and fists. She wasn't as strong as he, but she was fast, and when it came to it, she could punch harder than most men. She'd punched him often until the afternoon when the punches had become kisses.

Everything changed after that, and he was man enough to admit it was his fault. He'd been too aggressive, too hungry for passion. He'd frightened her, and she'd run from him straight to Liam. Not in a passionate way, but as if he were her life's purpose. She stopped helping her father make glass and began working in the castle. Within a year, she became chatelaine because everyone understood she would become mistress there when she and Liam wed.

Everyone, that is, except Liam who had plans of his own. And now that Liam was blissfully happy with a new bride, it was time for Connall to stake his claim. But rather than run to him, Mairi had run to London. It's how she made it clear that he was not the man for her no matter what he wanted.

Clear as MacAdaidh glass. She did not want him. So perhaps while wrapped in fevered misery, it was time for him to face the truth. Mairi was determined to find someone else, and he would do well to look to another woman. With his father likely to pass within the next few years, it was high time for him to marry and produce an heir.

Except the thought of someone other than Mairi left him sulky. He kept his misery to himself as much as he could, but there was no denying that he felt right sorry for himself. Feverish, travelling, and mourning a love that wasn't returned. Damned pitiful he was, and so he kept his mouth shut.

He did not tease the truth out of the women, he did not eat much for fear that it would come back up, and he never, not once, realized they were being robbed until the carriage stopped and the door was hauled open.

"Out ye come, lassies," the man said in a bad brogue. It was obviously fake, but the pistol was real. "One by one, easy now."

Connall didn't give them time. He launched himself forward, blankets and all, to tackle the bastard. There was only one shot in that pistol, and as expected, it went off with his attack. Even sick with a fever, Connall was quick, and he made sure the ball went wide. It shot a hole in his favorite carriage, but no one else was harmed.

He planned to beat the man senseless.

He got fouled in the blankets instead.

Worse, even though he bested the one man, he soon discovered there were three more with guns. Three *smart* thieves who hung back and laughed as he beat the man who'd opened the carriage door.

Eventually he escaped the confines of his blanket. Eventually, he rolled to his feet though he swayed with dizziness. And when he finally looked around, he saw the other thieves on their horses with their pistols pointed straight at him.

He lunged forward anyway and got a boot kick straight into his gut. Nausea overwhelmed him and he stumbled sideways. He would have still fought. Indeed, he'd gotten much worse damage during festival games. But he was ill, and his body rebelled. To his humiliation, he fell to his knees and began casting up what little was in his stomach.

"Out ye git," said the nearest one, his tone indicating he meant the women who still hid inside the carriage. At least that's what Connall thought he said.

"Don't hurt him. He's got a fever," said Sadie as she and her maid stepped out.

"I'll not touch a hair on his head," said the man on the horse, "if you give us your coins and jewels." Then he gestured to another who dismounted and approached, pistol at the ready. And why the hell couldn't he see clearly? Was it nearing dusk?

A quick look around told Connall that a man pointed a gun at the coachman, and that it was indeed nearing dark. As for options, he didn't see any. They were caught. He'd failed to protect his cousin, and why the hell hadn't he asked for Reuben to meet them in Edinburgh? The answer was sheer arrogance. His carriage and coat of arms were well known in Scotland. It would take an exceptionally bold highwayman to attack him on Scottish soil. But they weren't in Scotland, right now. They were at the northern tip of England, and he'd been a bloody idiot.

"I'll get you coin," he rasped. "Leave the ladies alone."

Too late.

The nearest bastard was already touching the maid. He lifted her chin and seemed to inspect a face that was tight with defiance. Made her look like Mairi, he thought. But then the villain scooped up a necklace and the gold pendant flashed in the sunlight.

"That's a pretty bauble," he said as he jerked it off her neck.

"No!" she cried, trying to grab it back. He shoved her away while Connall stumbled to his feet.

Damn it, he knew that necklace, as did most true Scots. Worse, he finally remembered the woman's face. Sadie's maid was none other than Iseabail Spalding, ward of the worst laird in Scotland. Baron Bain was crude, always looking for a fight, and kept his niece under lock and key. Hell, if her uncle found out that Connall had Iseabail, the man would waste no time in declaring war. And that was the last thing that anyone needed.

"Give it back!" he ordered the highwayman, though his voice was nearly as weak as the rest of him. He'd put all his strength into his fight with the one robber. Now he could barely stand. "I'll get you coin."

"Ye'll get us both," the man with the necklace responded. "Or we'll do much worse." He was still looking at Iseabail with hungry eyes.

"I'll get it!" Sadie said, her voice thick with hatred. "And be damned to you."

She turned to go back into the carriage. She knew where the secret compartment was. The one that contained all his coin in a small lockbox.

"Sadie," he rasped. "No."

He didn't care about the coin, but it was all he had to bargain with. Giving it over now would end any chance to negotiate. But he couldn't stop her. The best he could do was stagger between her and the nearest highwayman. Anyone who came near either of the women would get a taste of Connall's fists. At least until someone put a bullet in his brain.

He watched with dismay as Sadie slid open the hidden latch with a flick of her wrist. Odds were strong that the thieves would have found the compartment anyway, but it still hurt to see her grab the lockbox and hold it aloft.

"Here it is!" she called. Then she threw it with all her might, straight at the man on the horse.

The woman had strength, that was for sure. The box hit the bastard straight in the chest and he fumbled trying to catch it. Meanwhile, Connall launched himself at the thief with Iseabail's necklace, but the man was ready. He blocked Connall, then kicked out. Connall took the blow straight in his chest and still tried to grab the man's leg. He caught it, but it was a losing battle. He didn't have the strength he needed to—

Bang! Bang!

Connall tensed, expecting bullets to rip through his body. They didn't. Instead, he heard the thunder of hooves coming up the road fast. Were the bullets from the oncoming riders? He had no idea and no time to wonder as he scrambled for the thief with Iseabail's necklace.

He got a boot in the face instead, then the thief jumped on his horse and rode off. So did the others. His coachman had managed to punch his attacker in the face, but no more than that. By the time Connall recovered his breath, the thieves were gone, and they were quickly surrounded by...

Connall blinked in the evening gloom.

"Reuben?" he asked as he rubbed his aching jaw. "We're supposed to meet—"

"In Halifax, I know. But I got bored waiting for you and

thought to come up here." The man grimaced as he looked around. "Bold as brass, they are, to do this before full dark."

Connall agreed. At least the bulk of his coin was safe. When Sadie had thrown the thing, it had bounced off the thief to shatter on the ground. His purse was right now spilled into the dirt.

"How bad are you hurt?" Reuben asked as he jumped off his horse.

"My pride," he rasped as he leaned back against the carriage. "Ladies? Are you all—"

"We're fine," Sadie said. She was already on the ground picking up Connall's coins. She knew the value of what was spilled and would not let it go to waste. "Connall's got a fever. He's been sick since Edinburgh."

Reuben braced Connall against the carriage, then gently offered him a flask. "It's water, but I can get you something stronger."

Connall shook his head. Water would be all he'd manage for a bit now. God, he hurt. His head was pounding either from the thief's boot or his illness. "I'll be fine," he said, his eyes going to Iseabail. "Miss Spalding," he said. "Was that your necklace?"

Stupid way to ask it. Of course, she'd lost a necklace. He'd seen it happen. But was it *the necklace* or just a trinket?

The woman couldn't answer. She was trembling and her eyes were wet with tears. Damn. It must have been *the necklace*, the one that told one and all who she was. Without it, her uncle could cast her aside, say she'd died on the road to London, and keep her dowry for himself.

"Hey now," Reuben was saying as he gently came close to Iseabail. "What's your name, miss?"

Iseabail's eyes widened as the man came close to her and no wonder. Reuben was a huge man with thick muscle and a dark tattoo of a bastardized crest of London across his chest. It was the symbol of his control over areas of London best left unknown to women such as Iseabail. It was covered now, of course, but he couldn't hide his size or his sheer raw presence.

"Are you hurt?" Reuben asked.

She shook her head, but Sadie spoke up.

"He touched her."

Reuben made a noise akin to a growl, but then he kept his voice gentle. "It's a monster for sure who preys on women. But it was naught but a little rough up, yes?"

"Yes," Iseabail finally whispered as she straightened her spine. "I'm fine." Her voice broke on that last word and Reuben held out a hand to catch her should she fall. She didn't. But Connall knew the true reason for her anguish.

"He got her necklace, Reuban. The one that tells who she is."

"And just who is she?"

"A lady with a fat dowry and a brutal guardian."

Iseabail's gaze skipped to Connall. "You know?"

"Aye," he said as he let his gaze encompass Sadie. "But you should have told me."

His cousin stepped forward. "She needs to get out of Scotland. She's in danger up there."

Probably true, but by involving Connall, they'd endangered his clan as well.

"This necklace," Reuben pressed. "It's important?"

"Very," Connall answered. "It's the only way she'll get her dowry."

Sadie sighed. "And the only way she'll get married."

"Then I'll get it back for her," Reuben said. He was smiling, this rogue for hire, in that way all dangerous men do when they want to attract a pretty lady. Connall was too clean cut to accomplish the look, but Reuban had practiced flirtation from the moment he knew how to wink. He did so now as he turned all his charm onto Iseabail.

"She's the granddaughter of an earl," he said firmly. Or as firmly as he could given that he was very lightheaded.

Typically, that only interested the rogue more. "Always good to have the favor of a lady," he said as he gently raised Iseabail's hand and kissed it. It was a courtly gesture that wasn't lost on either woman. To see a man that large do the pretty was a sight that impressed every fair heart. And some of the darker ones as well.

"Damn it, Reuben…" Connall began. The man was a kingpin in the London underworld. He was not a good choice as a husband for anyone, least of all the granddaughter of an earl.

"My men will protect you down to London," Reuben said. The words were a command to his companions. "Me, I'm on a hunt for an heiress's necklace."

"I'm not an heiress," Iseabail said, her breath short.

"There's all sorts of treasure, my lady, and I'll bet you've got plenty to offer beyond gold." Then he bowed with exquisite style before jumping on his horse and riding away. Both women watched the man, their eyes wide and their mouths open.

"Don't even think about him," Connall commanded. "He's a rascal of the worst kind."

The three remaining men agreed. One even said, "A terrible choice for any gal."

Neither woman appeared to hear the warning.

CHAPTER SEVEN

London

M AIRI WAS PRACTICING talking the evening Connall returned
to London. She sat with the butler Parry and pretended he
was Prinny. Everyone thought that was a great joke because
Parry was thin and Prinny fat, but Mairi thought Parry's pompous
arrogance was spot on. The man sniffed as if she'd come from the
pigsty whenever her Rs rolled, and he sneered every time an O
sounded like AE. It was insulting, and yet she understood the
discipline needed to sound like an Englishwoman. As much as her
people clung to their hatred of the Sassenach, the English had a
disdain for the Scots. It was a fact of life, and if she meant to cross
the border to find a husband, then she needed to put her best
foot—or language—forward.

She really wanted to put her foot through Parry's sneering
mouth.

Fortunately for Parry's future ability to eat, the knocker
sounded, and he rose with a level of poise that made her despise
him more. He really was graceful, and she would do well to study
him, not hate him. But it had been a long ten days of constant
correction, and she was ill-tempered.

She slouched back on the settee and took childish glee in
allowing her knees to drift apart beneath her dress as she
sprawled in defiant exhaustion. She'd never done such a thing in

Scotland, and she was ashamed of her appearance now. And yet, she still did it.

"My heavens!" Parry exclaimed. That was as much as a scream from the man and Mairi perked up in interest. "But you cannot—" he began until a Scottish voice interrupted him.

"Aye, ye can and ye will. It's been a long, awful journey, and we're coming inside."

Mairi jumped to her feet, proving that she wasn't nearly as exhausted as she thought. "Sadie?" she called. Sure enough, the auburn-haired girl with the tight jaw and hard eyes was pushing her way inside. "Let her in, Parry," she commanded. "That's the duke's cousin—"

Her voice cut off as she saw Connall stumble against the doorframe. He was standing on his own—barely—and Sadie was clearing the way for a couple large men as they caught the duke and pulled him inside.

He looked like hell. His eyes were bright with fever, his skin flushed, and his handsome face was swollen on one side. Truth be told, he looked like a monster, but Mairi could only see injury and pain.

"Get him to a room upstairs," she commanded as if she were in charge in this house. "Parry, send for water and linen to tend his wounds." She looked at Sadie. "Has he seen a surgeon? Do his bones need to be set?"

"No," Connall rasped. "Naught's broken...save my pride."

He sounded even worse than he looked, his voice weak and distracted. And so, because that frightened her, she insulted him. That was how they'd always interacted. "There's nothing that can dent yer pride, Connall Aberbeag. I'm surprised that yer head could swell even larger than it already was."

He laughed, as she knew he would, and that sound reassured her. He had his wits, and after a blow to the head that was no small thing.

"Bring him along then," she said, waving to the two large men. "Upstairs to the nearest—"

"What's this?" the dowager countess called from the top of the stairs. "Parry, who are all these people?"

"It's the duke, my lady," Mairi said before Parry could answer. "With his cousin whom you promised to sponsor—"

"And my maid," Sadie said as if that made any difference.

"We were attacked by robbers," said the maid who, now that Mairi got a good look at her, was no maid at all, but that was for another time. She pointed to the men. "What are you waiting for? Upstairs with him!"

"My lady!" Parry called. "We're not prepared—"

"Good heavens! What happened to his face?" gasped the countess.

"Highwaymen," Mairi repeated, her heart beating hard in her throat as she said the words. "He needs to rest."

"But he was to take gentleman's quarters—"

"Here, my lady," she said, her tone hard. "He cannot recover without help, and no proper miss can go to his lodging."

The lady chewed her lower lip as she peered at Connall. "You'll not die, will you?" Her voice trembled with real fear.

"No, my lady," said Connall as he flashed a truly gruesome smile. "I'm not done in yet."

"Then I suppose I can let you rest here."

It was the permission Mairi needed to mobilize the staff. "Parry, see that a doctor is called immediately." She turned to glare at Connall before he objected. "Not a word of argument or I'll be ministering to your wounds myself. You know how I handle—"

"God forbid!" Connall groaned. "Fine. Waste the money on a sawbones."

"Set him in the room next to mine," she commanded. "It was the best one for a sickroom with a large window to air out the stink. Sadie, can you and..." She swallowed. She did not want to know right now why Iseabail Spalding was pretending to be a maid. "Can you share the bedroom across the hall?"

"Of course, we can."

"Do we need to call the Watch or tell someone about…" What did she know of how England handled their thieves?

One of the big men tugged at his cap as he guided Connall up the stairs. "That's been handled, miss. We stopped them afore evil could happen. The duke took the worst of it, but he kept his coin."

Mairi felt her gut clench. "He fought them over a few coins?" What an idiot to risk his life over a few pennies he could well afford. She'd be having a few choice words for him about that—

"He wasn't fighting because of the coin," Sadie said as she, too, headed up the stairs. "They started… One of them…" Sadie looked at Iseabail with sad eyes.

Oh dear. "Do either of you need a doctor?" Mairi asked with a lowered voice.

"No," Iseabail said. "One of the men—Mr. Reuben Bates— stopped him."

Then she would make pains to thank this Mr. Bates. But at the moment, she needed to see to Connall's care. She hadn't taken stock of the countess's sickroom supplies, but there had to be something. She looked at Sadie whom she knew to be a levelheaded woman, if rather dour thanks to her shrew of a mother. "Can you see that he's settled? Have them strip him down. I'll follow up in a minute with supplies."

Sadie nodded. "I'll see to it."

"Good. Parry, show me your liniments and whatever you have for fever."

Thankfully, after one quick glance at the countess, Parry didn't argue with her. He sent the maids scurrying to heat water and a footman to get the luggage. Then he gestured toward the housekeeper's room where Mairi had been working as she learned to how to organize staff and put on the countess's dinner party next week. It was to be her unofficial introduction to society. Right now, she shoved everything aside in order to get at a cabinet of medicines.

"This is it?" she asked looking at the meager contents.

"Yes."

She opened a jar and sniffed at it. This was not going to work. "I'll write down a list of things I need from an apothecary. You know of a good one?"

"Yes."

She scrawled out a list and handed it to him. "Send someone immediately." Then she gestured to a kitchen maid. "Bring soap and water now." She glanced back at Parry. "And brandy." She didn't wait to hear his reply as she headed upstairs.

She paused before entering the sickroom. She'd seen plenty of wounds and illnesses in her life and knew how even small cuts could turn ugly. A slight cough could mean a funeral two days later. It all depended on God, and so she whispered a prayer, squared her shoulders, and entered the room.

The men had done their job, and Connall lay beneath a sheet naked as the day he was born. Sadie was directing the placement of luggage—what little there was of it—and instructing the coachman to do what was needed with the carriage and its cargo.

Cargo? Oh yes. Liam's whisky. Mairi dismissed it from her thoughts as men's business. Her job was to take care of the man. And what a man he was. She could see from his outline on the sheet that he was as handsome a man as Scotland could make. Broad shoulders, narrow waist, long strong legs, and large feet. Every part exactly where it ought to be with no awkward angles or swollen joints. Healthy and attractive, and she was woman enough to see it.

She also saw that his breath was rapid and there was a sheen of sweat on his skin. His knuckles were scraped, and his hands shifted restlessly across the sheet. As for his face—well, one eye was swollen shut and his jaw purplish with a bruise, but he still had the wherewithal to smile at her, lopsided though it was.

"Have you come to tend to me?"

"I've come to slap that ugly grin off yer mouth." She sat down on the edge of the bed and began to wash the sweat and blood from his face. She touched him as gently as she could, wincing for him when she had to press hard. Typically, he didn't even blink.

"You look worried," he said softly. "I've been busted up worse by a ram, and well you know it."

"You didn't catch a fever from any sheep. And not one of them shoots a pistol." She swallowed, not wanting to imagine it, and yet needing to know the truth. "How many were there?"

"Four."

"And why would you fight over a few coins?"

He frowned at her. "You know me better than that."

Did she? Seemed to her that he often took pride in his wealth. At least he showed it to her often enough. Whenever he came to the MacCleal castle, he always bragged about what he'd bought in Edinburgh, what he'd dined on, and who had been his companion.

He sighed when he saw her face. "I was protecting the women," he said. "I'd have bested them all if I weren't already weak."

"Are you daft? You travelled with a fever?"

"The ladies need polish, Liam needs his whisky sold, and I wanted to see if the Scot had been beaten out of you yet."

"Never."

"Your words sound more English."

"I'm practicing."

"I don't like it."

She snorted. "And what's it to me what you like and don't like?"

His one eye stared at her. He looked like he wanted to say something. Flattery would be his usual words or some kind of tease. Not this time. There was a sadness about him that tugged at her and made her hand tremble.

"I'm done chasing ye, Mairi. I've shown you my heart and you've kicked it aside, so it's done now. I set you free to your Sassenach husband hunting." He sneered the words to make sure she understood his opinion of the men in England. "And I'll be looking for an English bride."

"What?"

"It's high time for me, don't you think?"

Well, yes it was. He was a future duke. It was long since time he found a wife. But somehow the realization that he meant to find a wife this Season shook her. "An' what's wrong with the Scotswomen? No Englishwoman can compete with—"

"You, Mairi. None can compete with you. And since we're done—"

"We never were!"

"Then I'll be finding a London rose."

It was what she wanted, right? For him to go on with his life just as she was moving on with hers. Except for his bruised and fevered body, this was what she wanted. Or so she told herself.

"Verra well," she said, her voice thick with her brogue. "But ye'll have to be able to stand if you mean to say yer vows." She pressed the cloth to the side of his neck. His flesh was hot with swelling and fever, and she watched his eyes flicker in thanks. "Rest now," she said. "There'll be plenty to discuss when ye wake."

His eyes drifted closed. He must have been fighting to stay awake for him to drop so fast. She kept washing him. That was a woman's duty when the man was ill, and she didn't trust his care to anyone else. She was just folding down the sheet to see to his chest when he spoke in a low rumble.

"I'll bet I find one afore you."

"What?"

"A bride before yer groom. A bet."

The man was half dead from fever and fighting, and he wanted to add to his pain? Fine. "A bet, then," she confirmed. "And what is yer forfeit?"

"A hundred guineas fer your dowry."

"What!"

He opened his good eye. "And if I wed first?"

She was still shocked, her mouth working without sound.

"I'll tell you what I want," he said, his breath coming fast.

"Glass, Mairi. I want ye to make me a full set of drinking glasses with yer own hand."

She couldn't promise that her new husband would let her back to Scotland to make his request, but she couldn't deny him either. "Done," she said. Especially since his coin was the only dowry she had.

CHAPTER EIGHT

I T TOOK TWO hours to cool Connall's body and he was awake
for fifteen minutes of it. He'd had the strength to make their
bet, then surrendered to sleep while Mairi tried to keep her mind
and her heart from declaring war on one another.

She cared for this man. A very great deal, if truth be told. And
who wouldn't want a handsome duke as a husband?

But now as always, the man was too much for her. She was a
strong woman. Some had even called her a firebrand. But in
every contest against this man, she'd lost. Even when she won a
bet—and she had won many—she always came out feeling like
the loser. She'd lose her common sense in doing everything to
win. She'd lose her health, her sanity, and her words in an all-
consuming war to keep him back, keep him away, and to prove
herself strong against him. But she wasn't strong when it came to
him, and pretending she was made her feel like a failure.

Simply put, he consumed her thoughts whenever he was
around. She'd learned young that such imbalance wasn't healthy,
and so she'd stepped away. She'd been promised to Liam at the
time, and so it was a necessary thing to leave Connall behind as
she focused on her future with Liam.

But now he was here and looking glorious in his sleep. Even
though a maid sat with her, helping her cool his overheated body,
Mairi could not keep her thoughts from turning lustful. He'd
touched her with his large hands. Nearly a decade ago, he'd

caressed her breasts with them, and she could still feel it. He'd pressed his lips to hers, he'd invaded her mouth with his tongue, and when she'd pulled away, he'd pursued her to lick her neck and jaw.

He'd said such things to her then. Called her "his bonnie lass" and other such nonsense. Then he'd pressed her down to the grass and she'd needed all her strength to shove him away and run. He hadn't fought her, though he could have caught her if he'd wanted to. The one she'd struggled with was herself. She knew what boys said about girls. She'd spent her childhood in the glass factory with her father hearing the crude talk of men. She'd be damned if she became one of their tales of conquest.

So she'd run and she'd cut him from her life in every way possible. If only the damned man would stay away! Instead, she was stroking every inch of his glorious body and wondering what it would have been like if she'd stayed all those years ago. What would she have felt? During their time together, what would they have done?

Afterwards would have been a humiliating disaster as he whispered about her to all his friends. But during? What would it have been like?

Those thoughts had tortured her for years and now she had even more images to add to her very graphic imagination.

In the end, she threw down the cloth with disgust. His body was cooler now, he was sleeping peacefully, so she had no need to sit here and torture herself by staring at his glory. She gathered up the dirty water basin and stomped out. She met Parry outside the bedroom door.

"Please have someone sit with him through the night. Get me immediately if his fever worsens."

The man's brows rose. "Doesn't he have a valet who can—"

"We're Scots. We don't need servants dogging our steps every second." She looked over Parry's shoulder at a footman loitering in the downstairs hallway. "Surely someone is interested in advancing himself. The duke will likely hire a manservant once he recovers and finds rooms in London."

Parry didn't react to her statement, but the footman did. He immediately leapt up the stairs and presented himself with a bow. "I should be happy to watch his grace through the night," he said.

"You?" Parry scoffed. "You can't stay awake through afternoon tea."

Mairi didn't care to hear the rest of the argument. She shoved the basin of dirty water at Parry. "Assign someone," she said. "I'm going to be..." She was about to say "in my bedroom," but she could hear voices in the room down the hall. The countess was grilling the newcomers. Now *that* was something she wanted to hear. She smiled at Parry. "I've a question for the countess," she lied as she headed for the female voices.

She knocked on the door but didn't wait to be invited in. She turned the knob and curtsied. It was very important to give the countess her due. The lady liked it even when it wasn't necessary.

"Is it all right that I join you?" she asked sweetly as she looked about the room. The countess was seated in a chair as she appeared to inspect Sadie's method of walking. Mairi recognized the drill. Walk, walk, walk, turn. Smile over your shoulder, mince sideways a bit, then return. She always felt like a show horse when doing that.

Meanwhile, standing in the corner with her head bowed like a servant, was Iseabail—the only lady born out of all of them. And what was going on with that?

"Come in," the countess said as she waved her in. "I've been putting Miss Allen through her paces. She'll have to join you in your lesson, I'm afraid, but all in all, she's much better prepared for a Season than I feared."

That was high praise coming from the countess.

"At least Lady Iseabail can speak without a brogue. Your mother was English, wasn't she?"

The countess frowned. "Lady who?"

She gestured to Iseabail whose eyes were wide with shock. "You know better than to come into a lady's house, ask for her help, all while pretending to be who you aren't."

The countess turned to Iseabail. "What is this? Who are you?"

Iseabail curtsied, her expression tragic. "Please, my lady, I'm Sadie's maid, nothing more. I only ask that I be allowed to serve as any other maid—"

Any other time, Mairi might have been more understanding. It was God's honest truth that Iseabail's situation was ugly. But a lie never made things better and if she wanted help, then by God, she'd be honest about it.

"She's Lady Iseabail. Granddaughter of the Earl of Spalding. Her father passed several years ago—"

"Poisoned by his brother," Iseabail said with tears glittering in her eyes.

"And now the ward of said brother."

"Goodness," the countess murmured. "It's *Hamlet*."

"Except I'm a woman and he means to marry me to his awful cousin. I had to get out. I had to!"

"Well, she wouldn't be a lady anyway. A granddaughter does not have the title."

Oh. Right. But with her airs and her heritage, everyone called her Lady Iseabail. Her uncle insisted.

Meanwhile, Sadie stepped forward. "It's true, my lady." She shot Mairi a hard glare. "She escaped and ran to me. I took her as my maid—"

"To do what?" Mairi rasped. Why could no one think their actions through? "Do you marry an English footman then? Will he get your dowry?"

The countess straightened up. "Dowry? What dowry?"

"Five hundred gold coins," Mairi said.

"I don't know that it's still there," Iseabail said, her voice tight. "My uncle probably spent them already."

"That is your groom's problem." The countess gestured Iseabail forward. "Come on. Head up. Step forward and let me look at you." She frowned. "Pretty face and the Scots call you a lady. That means a very great deal to some. I don't like the red hair and you're a Scot, so that weighs against you. Nevertheless, I think I can do something with you."

Sadie frowned. Clearly, she hadn't been around long enough to realize that the countess lived to matchmake. Her every thought was about a girl's assets on the Marriage Mart and how they could be promoted to best advantage.

Mairi folded her arms. "Do you mean to get married, Iseabail? It's the only way out from under your uncle's thumb."

The woman nodded. "But I haven't any money. How will I get dresses and hats? These aren't even my own shoes—"

"Tut." The countess waved her to silence. "There are ways around that." Her gaze cut across the room. "Three Scottish girls of modest means, and one with a title of sorts. Hmmm." She tapped her fingers on her lips. "I can do it," she said firmly. "If you listen to me. Every one of you must swear to do exactly as I say when I say it. Otherwise, you can leave my home now and do whatever poor people do when they have no possibility of better."

What were they to say to that?

"Of course, we will," they all said. And because Mairi had lived with the lady for longer than any of the others, she added an extra benefit for the lady.

"I'll teach them to run your household, too. Between the three of us, you won't have to lift a finger."

"Not a finger?" the woman cried. "Do you think it is easy to plan a come out? Of not one but *three* young ladies?"

"No, my lady."

"No!" she snapped as she stood up. "It is not. But mark my words, I'll see that you all get husbands and you'll be grateful for it." The woman headed for the door with a hard swish of her skirts. She appeared to be furious, but Mairi wasn't fooled. There was a martial gleam in her eyes and her lips twitched with pleasure. The countess adored nothing more than being a warrior in the social whirl.

Mairi opened the door for her as the lady sailed out. Then the woman paused in the hallway, looking back over her shoulder just as Sadie had been practicing a few moments before.

"Well, don't just stand there!" she said. "Downstairs, the lot of you. I'll see you three walking like ladies before bed tonight. And then tomorrow, the real work begins."

Sadie and Iseabail exchanged a startled look, then both rushed to follow. Mairi was the last to go, her heart and her mind still torn. Her mind told her to follow smartly. She was a prize as a wife, and some lucky Sassenach was going to be grateful for her. But her heart still lingered down the hallway with Connall. What if his fever spiked? What if he grew delirious?

What if he woke and decided that marrying Lady Iseabail was the best choice for him? The woman knew how to run a household, was a titled Scotswoman, and she was *right here*. What if he picked her? That was an unsettlingly close possibility.

"Miss MacAdaidh!" the countess called from down the stairs. "I will not tolerate dawdlers. Do you come and learn how to be a lady? Or do you—"

"Coming!" she cried as she rushed forward. "I thought to check on the duke's health."

The woman frowned. "Is he ailing?"

"No more than before."

The woman pressed her lips tight as she looked toward Connall's room. She was worried, though about what, Mairi had no idea. Did she fear for Connall's survival or fear having illness in the house? Either way, she had a practical mindset that Mairi appreciated. "Does he need more attention?" asked the countess.

"No, my lady."

"Then come down here and learn something!"

"Yes, my lady."

And so it was done.

CHAPTER NINE

C ONNALL WAS FEELING more like himself. He'd spent nearly two days wrapped in a fever, but it had broken yesterday afternoon. Since then, he'd slept well and was now bathed and shaved, thanks to the help of a very ambitious footman in the countess's household. Lloyd was his name, and Connall had been so exhausted by his illness that he never figured out if that was the man's given name or surname.

Damn, but he was tired. He'd always thought the English way of dressing was tiresome, but it never left him weak as a kitten. That meant he was back in bed—barely dressed—and staring at the ceiling as he thought about Mairi. He could hear the noises of the household and knew that the ladies were having a dancing lesson. The strains of the music filtered to him up here. So he lost himself in a vision of Mairi in a sweeping gown, dancing amid the glow of a thousand candles.

She was always associated with fire in his mind. She'd been raised beside the furnace of her father's glassworks, but he'd never seen her as fragile as glass. She reminded him more of the copper his clan mined. She was beautiful and powerful like any metal, but still flexible enough to bend to whatever life threw at her. He admired that in her and dreamed of heating her passion—

A knock sounded at his door, interrupting his reverie. Good thing too, since he'd sworn two days ago to give up all thoughts of Mairi.

"Come in," he called, hoping it was her. She'd checked on him twice during his fever, cooling his body with a soothing cloth, and then once this morning to declare his fever gone. Every time he'd tried to tease her, but she'd bid him sleep and he'd sunk deeply into that place where all was rest while she soothed his body. He hoped now to give a better account of himself. Except when the door opened, he saw a woman with fiery red hair and the dot of freckles.

"Lady Iseabail," he said, doing his best to hide his disappointment. "Shouldn't you be at the dancing lesson?"

"We finished that and have been sent to do our chores."

His brows rose. "Chores?"

"Mairi and Sadie are learning how to balance accounts for a household."

Connall frowned. "They already know. Sadie's been managing for her mother—"

"Sadie knows how to track a small home with few servants and a flock of sheep. Mairi has managed an entire castle. Neither has hosted a dinner party in London."

He had to acknowledge her point. "Then why aren't you—"

"I am to speak with you."

He didn't like being put in the category of a chore, but he could understand that some discussions were difficult. And Iseabail had never seemed like a woman who rushed into unpleasant things. She more than any of them knew how unpleasant a person's life could get.

"Then come on. Out with it. What is it—"

"Do you mean to take a wife this Season?"

That was putting it bluntly, but then the Scots could be a forthright people. And he would do well to answer in kind, though it would lead to a very difficult conversation with her. "Yes, Iseabail, I do."

"And you're no longer set upon Mairi?" she pressed.

"That's correct," he said. Then he waved her inside before sitting up more fully in bed. "Shut the door, Iseabail. It's time we spoke clearly, you and I."

She looked momentarily panicked, but then straightened her shoulders as if she were the Queen of England. "It is not proper for me to be here alone with you." She spoke in clear, unaccented tones and he was startled by how perfectly she mimicked a cold Sassenach lady.

"My apologies," he said, matching her cool tone. "But you did come in here to my sickbed. I thought you would appreciate privacy for the coming discussion."

She frowned at him. "Your Grace..." she began, then became lost for words as she said no more.

He sighed and sat up as straight as if he were having an audience with a royal even though he sat in a bed and wore little beyond the evening jacket Lloyd had found somewhere. "Lady Iseabail, leave the door open for propriety's sake, but please bring a chair close so that we may converse quietly."

She nodded, left the door wide, then sat in the chair furthest away from him. Certainly, he thought wryly, he'd love to shout his romantic intentions across the room. But then he moderated his irritation. For all that he was in a sickbed, she was frightened of being alone with him. He'd been around enough women to know when they relished catching him alone in a dark corner, and when they flinched at the very sight of his large hands. Iseabail had too much pride to flinch, but she was certainly afraid of being alone with a large man. Even as she stiffened her spine and faced him square on, she kept an escape route open for her to run away if necessary.

"I'll not hurt you, Iseabail," he said gently.

"But will you marry me?" she asked.

He stared, momentarily taken aback. He'd had various encounters with her over the years and had thought her to be a reserved and generally frightened girl. She didn't run free the way Mairi had, even as a child. Mostly because her mother had held a tight rein over her, but also because the women of the Bain clan were cowed creatures who kept their heads down and their mouths shut. He would never have guessed she'd be this bold. But then, he'd never guessed she'd run across Scotland to hide as Sadie's maid.

In the face of his silence, Iseabail pressed her point. "The countess has been telling us to evaluate our place on the Marriage Mart dispassionately. Therefore, let me tell it to you. My mother was English and taught me well. You are a duke, and it would do you good to have an English seeming wife."

"I'm a Scotsman," he growled.

"And I am a Scotswoman. Our clans have been friends through the years. An alliance would do well between us."

"We have been friends," he said gravely. "But marrying you would set us at war with your uncle, and well you know it."

"I do." At least she wasn't trying to hide that fact. "But he would lose in a fight with the Aberbeag, and he knows it. You've done well with alliances and in trade."

"Your uncle is a man gripped by moods. Neither of us can guess what he knows or what he will do."

She bit her lip but didn't argue the point. "I am the grand-daughter of an earl, you will be a duke. Our titles are well matched."

"And titles mean little to me. It is the woman I will marry, not her ancestry."

She arched a brow. "It's your title that all the other women will want. I know you to be a good, honorable man."

He hadn't thought her words could cut him, but they did. Not because she was accusing him of anything, but because she didn't know the truth. "Iseabail," he said gently, "what do you know of your father's death?"

Her face paled in surprise, but it didn't stop her from speaking. "He was poisoned," she said firmly. "By my uncle."

So she did know some of it. "Do you have any proof of it?"

She shook her head. "My mother said he was poisoned. Said it was clear from the way he died."

"But you don't know who did it—"

"My uncle wanted charge of the clan."

"Which is not proof."

She pressed her lips tightly together and jerked her chin down. She knew she had no proof, only guesses. Which made what he was about to say even worse.

"Do you know where your uncle might have gotten the poison?"

"No," she said, her voice very hushed.

He looked down, unwilling to meet her gaze while he spoke. What he was about to say would give her no comfort and him even less, but it had to be done. "When I was a boy, I liked to hide in the castle. I loved to climb and was good at finding all sorts of places to sit and listen to what the adults said and did."

"Boys are permitted such freedoms," she said, somewhat bitterly.

"Aye. And on this day there was a lot to hear and see as your clan was visiting."

She leaned forward. "Was it a fair day?"

"No. A hunting party come to rest for the night."

"That's a long way for our hunters to go to end up at your castle."

"Aye." He took a deep breath, but she made her guess before he could speak.

"You overheard my uncle plotting."

"No." He said the word forcefully. His life would be easier if he had heard such a thing. "I heard talk of poisons between your uncle and my father."

Her body went completely still. "Your father helped—"

"I don't know." He sighed. "I was a boy. I heard them speaking about copper mining and the poisons it can create."

"He got them from your father!" she gasped.

"I don't know!" he said, doing his best to be forceful without shouting. "They only spoke of arsenic, not of using it. Certainly not of one giving it to the other."

She narrowed her eyes. "But you suspect something?"

His expression flattened out. "When I heard about your father's death—about the nature of it—I asked my father if it sounded like arsenic poisoning to him. He grew furious as I have never seen him. He beat me for my impudence. He said I must learn that accusing a man of murder is a thing that can never be done lightly."

She rose up from her chair. "But you didn't accuse anyone, did you?"

"I didn't."

"And did your father—"

"He never spoke of it again, though I asked."

Her eyes widened. "You asked again?"

"Once when I began doing our business negotiations. We've had a profitable exchange with your clan." Her clan had coal and his had copper. Truthfully, he needed the relationship with her uncle more than he needed a wife. "I asked why we go far out of the way to get coal when your mine is so close."

"Because my uncle demands a high price—"

"Not from us."

She jolted at that.

"The coal comes to us at a generous cost, but my father will buy no more than absolutely necessary."

"Because he helped kill my father."

"Because he does not trust your uncle."

She stepped forward until she gripped the post at the base of his bed. "But he knows."

"He will not speak of it."

"You have to ask—"

"I have. I asked him bluntly if your uncle had taken arsenic from us…" He stopped speaking when she visibly flinched. Her knuckles went white, and he waited until she steadied.

"And?" she finally whispered.

"He cuffed me. I was larger and stronger than he, and old enough to win a battle against my father. But in this, he would not be cowed. And he repeated what he had said years before."

"That one cannot accuse a man of murder without proof."

"And support, Iseabail. Your uncle is a laird who sells coal to Edinburgh. He has a great many people who will defend him."

She nodded slowly though her grip never released on the bedpost. "And so you will not marry me for fear of angering my uncle."

He snorted. "Had I the proof, I would do everything to right the injustice. I have nothing but the vague memory of a boy." He touched the cold back of her hand. "I will not marry you, Iseabail, because every time you look at me, you will think of your murdered father. And I think the same whenever I see you."

Her eyes widened then, and she drew her hand away from him. Not quickly, which reassured him, but with a slow withdrawal and a lifted chin. "I hate Scotland," she rasped. "My uncle poisons everything there."

"Then you hate the man, not the country."

She shrugged, and he could tell that it was one and the same to her.

"I cannot help you with your uncle. I would if I could. But I can do something else." It was the least he could do, and it would go a long way to easing his guilt over whatever had happened years ago between his father and her uncle. "I will pay for your come out, Iseabail. That's the real reason you came here, isn't it? You need someone to pay for the countess's sponsorship."

She shrugged. "The countess has pointed out to all three of us that you will be the biggest catch this Season for all that you're Scottish. A duke is a duke, she said, and we would all be extravagantly fortunate to become a duchess."

He sighed. He had no interest being pushed as this Season's most eligible bachelor, but he knew it would happen. Instead, he focused on her. "We would not suit, Iseabail."

"I know!" she cried, still fighting hard to control her emotions. "I hadn't before, but now..." She took a deep breath and released the bedpost. "Now, I know."

"But I will pay for your come out," he repeated. It was an

extravagant offer. He had already agreed to pay for Sadie's gowns, not to mention the gold coins he'd promised to Mairi, but he could not leave a woman to face Baron Bain alone. She needed help, and he could afford it, though it might pinch his ready coin. "Iseabail, you are as much a catch as I. A lady for all that you're Scottish."

"Not as good a catch," she said bitterly. "I am a woman and therefore powerless."

"No Scotswoman would say such a thing. You have strength, Iseabail. If you didn't, you wouldn't be here now. You'd be married to—"

"Enough," she snapped. "I know where I am and what I have to do." She lifted her chin and gave him a shallow curtsy. "Thank you, Your Grace, for the coin." Then she fled the room.

He stared at the doorway where she had disappeared and cursed himself for not being a god. He was a Scotsman and a future duke, but he was unable to find and punish the man who had killed her father. And while he cursed himself for his failures, the one person he'd wanted to see stepped into the empty door.

"Connall," Mairi said. "I didn't know."

"No one knows," he groused. "That's the problem."

She nodded as she crossed to his bedside and pressed her hand to his cheek. It wasn't a tender gesture. She was checking for fever, but he gripped her fingers nonetheless. "I cannot help her," he said as failure pressed in on him.

"You're paying her bills," Mairi returned. "I'd say that's more than anyone else would do."

"And if my father helped to—"

"Do you truly think that?"

He swallowed and shook his head. "Not on purpose. Not knowing what would happen."

She curled her hand beneath his chin, lifting his face to hers as she settled on the coverlet beside him. "Then the fault lies with her uncle," she said. "It always has."

There it was. The one thing Mairi did better than any other.

She cut through chaos to do what must be done. And when there was naught that could be done, she cut through the emotions to say what was true.

"The fault is with the poisoner," he said. "Whoever that is."

"Which is not your father, and it is not you."

How freeing to hear those words spoken aloud. "I still feel bad for her."

"Ach, Connall, you feel all manner of things all the time, and none of it makes more than a piss in the wind's difference."

Her crude words startled a laugh out of him. Trust Mairi to find the right way to pull him out of his darker mood. "What I feel," he said catching her wrist and using it to pull her forward, "is a great deal better than I did yesterday."

"That's thanks to my nursing, I'll have you know."

"I do," he grinned. "And now I mean to reward you." Which he did by pulling her close for a kiss.

CHAPTER TEN

L ORD, SAVE HER from a man who knew how to kiss.

Mairi had known the kiss was coming. She'd seen the intention in his eyes long before he cupped her cheek and pulled her in. What surprised her was her own willingness to savor every second of it. She didn't move away, and she didn't stop him. Instead, she reveled in the way his lips teased hers before the sudden thrust of his tongue between her teeth. And when she melted into the kiss, he touched every part of her mouth in a wild thrust and parry of dance.

Damn, he was good.

She'd been kissed by other men. He was her first, though, so many years ago. Then as she grew older, she allowed a few others to try. Several kisses occurred beneath mistletoe. A few beneath a romantic night sky. And one had been a shock from a man who received a shock of his own when her knee struck between his thighs.

None of those kisses, including her very first, held a candle to this one.

She rolled her tongue around his, she felt her breath grow short as her heart speeded up. By the time she realized she was clutching his upper arms, she abruptly shoved him away.

Too much!

"Mairi." Her name was spoken in a soft tone, half growl, half whisper. There was a gentleness in it that she couldn't deny, even as her mind flashed memories of their first time. He'd been hard and fast, nothing had felt right, and she'd run, run, run.

She pushed to her feet to do so again, but he caught her hand. She could have broken his hold, but she'd spent most of her life learning how to stand her ground. Why would she run away now? Damn it, she couldn't make sense of her own illogic.

"Mairi, won't you stay for a moment?"

"What is there to say?" she countered, her tone more biting than she intended. They were the only words that came to mind. She was too busy trying to calm herself to manage anything more than casual hostility.

"That I'm not the callous boy I used to be," he said. "That I know better how to treat a woman."

She swallowed. Her heart was beating too fast for her to control, and she needed to run or fight or something—anything— to keep herself from tearing apart. "I know what you've learned and who with. I swear the whole of Scotland knows."

"And what is that, do you think?" he challenged. "In the last ten years, what have I done to make you fear me?"

"I'm not afraid!" she lied. Well, she wasn't afraid of him, per se, but of what he made her feel. Why wouldn't her heart slow down?

"Then will you look at me?"

She turned to stare at him. She had to work herself up to his face, so she started with his chest, his ruddy chest hair revealed in the vee of his evening jacket. She saw the dark flush to his skin along his neck. His jaw was square, his mouth… She jumped her gaze up from his mouth. His eyes were steady and clear, but his expression was troubled as he watched her.

"Who hurt you?" he asked. "Who made you fear a man's touch?"

"Don't be daft," she said as she wrenched her wrist free from his grasp. "Yer the only one who took what I didn't give. Except one, and I paid him harshly for his mistake."

He grinned. "Was that Seamus, three Christmases ago?"

Her brows rose. "You heard of that?"

"We heard. And if he weren't still speaking soprano, I would have made sure he never forgot—"

"I can protect myself," she snapped.

"Aye," he said. "But when will you stop protecting and allow a man to—"

"Have me?" she interrupted. "When I've a ring on my finger and have sworn my duty to my husband before God."

"And you think you will surrender then?" He shook his head. "I think it will take a very determined and very patient man to breach those walls of yours."

"You'll never know, then will you?" It was a childish taunt unworthy of the woman she thought she was. But apparently, this man could bring her back to her pre-teen days of taunts and petty rivalries when she'd bested him in high jumps, but not much else.

She calmed herself by smoothing her skirt. "I best be getting back to the countess." Then she gasped, belatedly remembering why she'd come up here. "I forgot to ask, will you be up and dressed for her dinner party in two nights? She's got a bevy of girls for you to charm."

His brows arched in surprise. "A whole bevy. My, my. Good thing I have plenty of charm."

"So you think," she drawled. "Well? Will you?"

He nodded. "I could do it tonight, if I must. I've got clothes on order that Lloyd can get for me. And he'll—"

"You'll retire to your gentleman's rooms tomorrow then?" she interrupted. "No need to stay here."

His expression tightened. "I can. Although…" he said, a canny look crossing his features. "If I'm to cover the expenses of two girls now, perhaps it'll be best that I remain here. Save some coin."

"You've plenty of coin," she retorted.

"Aye, but if I'm to save for your wedding gift, then I've got to be careful."

He was teasing her. She could tell by the way he cocked his head to the side and made as if to wink, but then didn't. She'd caught him once practicing the look in the mirror, and here it was again. Perfected, now, and damned if it didn't work a little on her.

"You'll have to talk to the countess about that," she said tartly. "It makes no difference to me where you sleep, except that I'll have to adjust the food planning. You eat more than a horse."

He grinned at her then waved her away. "Go on then. Send Lloyd to me as it seems I must be presentable sooner rather than later."

She sniffed and left, her belly in a knot. It had been hard enough to block him from her mind when he was sweating with fever. How was she going to forget him when he was awake and flirting? Especially when all she had to do was think of him and her lips burned with the memory of his kiss?

CHAPTER ELEVEN

T WO DAYS LATER the house was filled with excitement. Everyone was happy except Mairi who was too busy to be anything but annoyed. Truthfully the servants were well trained and except for a last minute change to the menu, everything appeared to be going exactly as it should. The silver was polished, the table was set to perfection, and all of them had new clothes for the occasion, even the countess.

But with everyone so chipper and with no one to yell at in the kitchen, Mairi found her mood growing tighter and darker. The countess had grilled them all on the gentlemen attending this night. She'd even selected who would be the best husband for each of them and made sure the seat assignments matched. Mairi was given a second son of modest means but excellent breeding. He had significant musical talent, a fondness for the law, and enjoyed political entertaining. The last bit was the important part. He was a man who would likely need a wife who could throw together parties large and small without notice, and since Mairi had done so well with tonight's planning, the countess thought she would make the best wife for him.

She couldn't remember the man's name. In her mind, she called him Second Rate Barrister even though he had no official law training.

It was time to dress, so Mairi made it upstairs only to pause on the landing. To the right was Connall's bedroom, and she could hear his muted laughter through the bedroom door. She had no idea what he was amused by, only that he and his man Lloyd seemed to be getting along very well. The sound set off two completely contradictory feelings inside her.

His chuckle told her on a deep level that all was well. She knew he took his responsibilities seriously, but he'd always been one to smile when things were good. His laughter meant that things were very good at the moment, and she could relax.

But as soon as she did, the opposite thoughts burned through her brain. All was good for the man because he was rich, titled, and about to be buried beneath a tide of women who would do anything to become his duchess. She, on the other hand, had no dowry, no title, and no future unless she secured a man as soon as possible. Of course, all was well with Connall. That didn't mean all was well with her.

She turned her back on his laughter and headed for her bedroom. But then she heard the girls giggling. Truthfully, Sadie was not a girl who giggled ever. Her mother had been the worst kind of shrew, and now Sadie was enjoying herself with Iseabail in a giggles-throughout-the-night kind of way. The two girls had stuck together like peas in a pod and were excited for their first presentation to society.

She didn't blame them for their happiness. She envied them. Mairi had never had a sibling, much less a sister. The closest she'd ever come was when she first started work at the castle. She'd been one of two girls set to sleep in the kitchen to keep the fire burning through the night. She had a blissful month with a new friend until her father had woken up to the dangers of a girl on the lowest rung of the castle hierarchy. All of the laird's men had access to the kitchen, and though nothing had happened to her, few kitchen maids could say the same. At least until she became chatelaine.

So young Mairi had returned to her cot above the glassworks and had slept there until she'd run away to London three weeks ago. To hear Sadie and Iseabail giggle now created a longing inside her that left her hollow. Did she dare try to fill it by knocking on their door? The other two were clearly good friends, what would they want with her?

If she were at home, these feelings wouldn't ever arise. There was always so much work that she could distract herself with one task or another. But here, she needed new friends, and so she took the risk.

She knocked gently on their door. The laughter immediately ended and Mairi felt bad for stopping their fun. Then Sadie opened the door.

"Were we too loud?" she asked.

"What? No, why would you think that?"

She looked back at Iseabail who was sitting at the mirrored vanity. "We are just very excited," she said quietly. They didn't look excited. They looked afraid and nervous with a dash of giggling hysterics. Especially when Iseabail tried to put a decorative comb in her hair and ended up pushing her braid out of place giving her a lopsided look. The girl half sobbed, half laughed in dismay. Sadie, too.

"We've been trying for an hour to figure out what to do with these combs," she said, gesturing to another one with a long, long feather sticking out the side. "Didn't the countess give you one, too?"

"I don't know," she said. "I have been—"

"—running the kitchen," Sadie said. Then she clapped her hands on her cheeks. "You aren't even dressed!"

"There's still time—"

"If you hurry! Come on! Let's see how your dress looks."

Sadie pushed her back out the door. She wasn't rough at all, but she crowded Mairi until she had no choice but back away. Iseabail, too, abandoned her hair and hurried to back up Sadie. Before long, the two women had chided and teased Mairi into her own bedroom.

"Oh, look how pretty your dress is!" Sadie said the moment she stepped into the room.

"And you have a comb, too!" Iseabail cried. "It's from the countess and it... it... well it matches, doesn't it? I mean, the feathers are lovely and so colorful."

Colorful was one word for it. Feathers were often used as decoration, but these were painted bright colors. At least three of them were a faded kind of red which would kind of match her pink dress. Mairi looked at it in dismay. "I'm supposed to put that in my hair?"

Iseabail nodded. "We all have one. It was a nice gesture from her."

How was she going to put that thing in her hair? She'd never been more grateful to have dark, boring hair. At least she wasn't a redhead like Iseabail. That thing would clash horribly.

"Don't think about it," Sadie said. "Get dressed. We'll figure out the combs somehow."

The two girls helped her change, each taking a hand in pulling her stays tight. She was a strong woman capable of blowing glass and cleaning a carcass for a feast. She did not have a tiny waist and she despised the need to plump her breasts as well. But she was trying to attract a man who needed her to run a London household. That did not usually include having the muscles to haul a stag onto a spit, so she would hide the strength in her form.

With Sadie and Iseabail's help, she tightened her ribs down and created cleavage in front. She pulled on a pink dress when she was definitely not a woman fond of pale colors. Then Iseabail retrieved the two paint pots given for the three of them to share. Mairi wasn't going to put anything on her face, but Iseabail knew what to do. She rimmed Mairi's eyes with charcoal and made her cheeks more rosy than ruddy.

Mairi peered into the mirror. "Goodness," she murmured, echoing the countess's favorite exclaim. "I look like a girl."

Sadie laughed. "That's what you want, isn't it?"

She wasn't sure. "I mean, I look like those girls who put flowers in their hair and giggle when a boy looks at them."

"That means you look young and fresh. And you don't have

to giggle if you don't want to." Sadie took her hand and spun her around to face Iseabail who was watching them with serious eyes. "What do you think?"

Iseabail tilted her head left and right before a slow smile warmed her face. "I think you are so used to stomping around brutish men that you never learned how to be a girl. And by that, I mean young and giggly."

Mairi winced. "I'll never giggle."

"Want to bet?" Iseabail challenged.

"What?"

"Sit down," she said as she pulled out the chair to the vanity. "I'll bet I can make you giggle inside of five minutes."

Mairi snorted, making sure it was a very masculine, very loud sound. "Not possible."

"I bet it is." She grabbed the brush off the table and began to straighten Mairi's curls. Her strokes made Mairi wince, but she'd suffered worse at her father's hands when she was little. Once the worst of the knots were out, Iseabail began to braid the front part of her hair up while the back fell in gentle waves. "How do you want it done up top? A bun, crisscross, or—"

Sadie and Mairi answered at the exact same instant with the exact same words.

"Just keep it out of my eyes."

Mairi's startled gaze locked with Sadie's through the mirror. "I am not that predictable," she said.

"You are," Iseabail said as she twisted the braids around. "It comes from being raised by men. Believe me, I know."

"But you're very girly!" Sadie exclaimed.

"My mother died only recently. If it weren't for her—"

"You'd be like me?" Mairi asked, her tone only half teasing. She didn't like to think she was deficient in any way, much less in being female. But it would be stupid to deny the truth. Up until a few weeks ago, she was a person who worked and who already had a husband selected for her. She'd been set to marry Liam and all he'd care about was how well she managed his home. Which is what she'd done to perfection. Now he was married to someone else, and she was suddenly adrift without a feminine wile.

"You're naturally beautiful," Iseabail said. "Just remember to smile. You've got a scowl that sets the footmen shaking in their boots, but you're trying to attract a husband tonight."

She scowled at herself in the mirror. After all she'd done to become the most capable woman around, what she really needed was to know how to be a simpering girl. "This is not going to work," she moaned.

"Of course, it will," Sadie said. Then when Mairi turned desperate gazes on her, the girl shrugged. "At least you won your bet. No giggles."

"Not yet," said Iseabail as she picked up the feathered monstrosity. "So, where shall we put this?"

"I have no idea."

"Well, let's just see, shall we?" She began first by pushing the comb up the side of her face, causing the feathers to flap distractingly out the side of her head like a growth.

"Not that!" she gasped.

"Yes, that does look odd. How about this?"

She tried setting it along the top of her head to rest backwards like a hat. It seemed fine at first because she couldn't see it, but the moment she tilted her head down it looked like a bird's nest sat in the center.

"That's very strange," she said.

"Very strange," Sadie agreed, "but you are rather tall for a woman. Maybe no one will see it."

"Connall's taller than I am. He'll tease me mercilessly about it."

Iseabail pulled it out then set it to the back of her head. "How about this?"

Even though most of it was hidden behind her head, several strangely colored feathers stuck out like gills from her neck.

Sadie laughed. "You look like a feathered fish." Then she

pursed her lips like a fish mouth and set her hands along the side of her neck, waving her fingers like fins. It was the silliest thing Mairi had seen in a long time and laughter bubbled up inside her.

"Ah hah!" cried Iseabail as she pointed her finger at Mairi. "You giggled! I won!"

"I did not!" Mairi cried. "I laughed. That's different."

"Really?" Iseabail challenged. "We'll see about that." Then she began to put the feathered comb in all sorts of ridiculous directions and places. At one point, she used it to tickle Mairi's nose and suddenly all three of them were giggling like children. Indeed, she was laughing so hard, she was grateful for the stays for holding her sides in tight.

But oh, it felt so good.

"What's this? What's this?" the countess demanded as she swept into the room. "Everyone here and looking lovely! Goodness, Mairi, what have you done with that comb? It looks like a jungle frog landed on your face."

Mairi had no idea what that meant. Who had ever heard of a jungle frog? But the very idea of that had her laughing anew. And once she did, the other two did, too, until the countess herself dropped her hands on her hips and grinned at them all.

"It's so good to hear laughter in this house again!" she exclaimed.

And when they settled down, Sadie attempted a question. "Countess, what is a jungle frog?"

"What? Oh, it's something Gwen used to talk about. Apparently, they've got long legs, long toes, and are wildly colorful. She knows all sorts of bizarre things. We never knew what she was talking about half the time, but something about colorful things in a mishmash became a jungle frog to me." She waved Iseabail away from the vanity. "Now, let me fix this thing. Really, I don't know how you could imagine wearing it so that it flops over your eyes."

"It's my fault," Mairi laughed. "I can't keep my head still."

"No, I can see that," the lady said seriously. Then she pointed at the other girls. "Go on. Get yours. I'll show you how you're meant to wear them."

And with that she began to pull and re-pin Mairi's hair, setting the braids to one side of her head while the colored feathers lay on the opposite side seeming to hold the upswept design in place. It was a marvelous effect, and the colors added a beautiful touch.

"I don't like painted feathers," the countess mused. "They're all the rage, but I can see now that it's not as attractive as I thought. I still think this works, though. Unless you'd prefer something simpler?"

"I...I don't know," Mairi said as she gazed at herself in the mirror. "I've never... I don't look like this normally."

"Well, of course you don't. What use would it be in the wilds of Scotland? But you're in London now, and I think you look lovely."

She had to take the lady's word for it. She couldn't credit that the painted, feathered woman in the mirror was herself. There was nothing there that she connected with. Not the hairstyle or the pink cheeks. Certainly not the full bosom or the shimmery pink gown. And yet, part of her did feel pretty.

"I don't ever wear pink," she said softly, not by way of criticism, but more because she felt like she was expanding herself. Suddenly, she was someone new and—

"Well, that's a new side of you," drawled a Scottish voice from the doorway.

Mairi spun around and was surprised that neither her hair nor the comb went flying. All was secure except her heart as she saw Connall framed in the doorway in his London finery. No trace of his illness remained. Indeed, his skin looked flushed and healthy, especially his wicked smile. His shoulders were always broad, but in a black jacket that fitted him to perfection, he looked every inch a duke. There was more to his clothing, all well made and showing off how fine a body he had, but Mairi could not think of anything beyond the way he looked at her.

Appreciation shone through his eyes. The cleavage, no doubt, was the cause. And yet, his gaze seemed to take in all of her.

"Feeling strange, aren't ye?" he asked, his brogue very thick. "Myself as well. These are not the things we're used to, is it?"

She shook her head. "Not at all."

"It's beautiful, you are. I wish your father could see it."

She felt her cheeks heat. Yes, her father would be surprised to see her dressed as such. He often moaned that he hadn't the knowledge to teach her womanly things. "Your father would be proud of you too," she said.

He answered by running his hands down his jacket and puffing out his chest. "I feel like I've been trussed up like a goose in all this finery. I miss my plaid."

"There won't be an English girl able to handle you," she said. Or a Scottish lass for that matter. He was too handsome for his own good, and well he knew it.

"I don't mind. I'll be too busy keeping the Sassenach men from trampling you in their ardor. You'll turn their heads."

This was uncomfortable for her. She wasn't used to his compliments or that look in his eye. But she couldn't deflect it with an insult. Not in this dress. It made no sense, but she felt like their usual banter could only be done by the usual Mairi. But now she was this new person in a pink dress with painted feathers on. Who knew what she would say to a flirtatious Scot? And while she stood in awkward silence, the countess grew impatient.

"Enough of staring at each other. You're both pretty as can be, though a duke should be more reserved. Go on now. Let me fix the other two." She waved Connall away and gestured the girls inside. Mairi stepped into the back corner of the room because she wasn't ready to head downstairs. It was so strange, but she was trying to embrace strangeness.

What she'd learned so far was this London Mairi sometimes wore pink, could giggle like a young girl, and did not know how to insult a gorgeous Scot. It wasn't enough to build a future upon, but it was a start. And so with that thought fixed in her mind, she faced the evening ahead with a flutter in her stomach.

Was that excitement? Anxiety? An ailment?

She had no idea. But whatever it was, she was sure to find out soon. They had less than fifteen minutes before the guests were set to arrive. And though she could have spent it downstairs checking on the food one last time, she decided to stay here instead. She wanted to see what the countess did with Sadie and Iseabail's headpieces. And she wanted to squeeze their hands, smile at their reflections in the mirror, and face their very uncertain futures together.

London Mairi was about to have a glorious evening.

CHAPTER TWELVE

CONNALL HATED ENGLISH clothes. They were heavy and itched. The cravat constricted his throat, and the jacket was so tight that he might rip it should he do anything but eat or drink in the slowest possible manner.

But he liked the way Mairi's eyes had widened when she took in his attire. And he definitely noticed the way she touched her lips as if remembering their kiss. She did it discretely, but he saw and if that was the result of this thrice-damned itchy attire, then it was worth it.

The dinner went better than most of these affairs. The countess kept a lively discussion going throughout the evening while still giving every person a chance to shine. It was obviously a matchmaking evening as everyone except for the countess was on the hunt for a spouse. He was seated between a woman who excelled in gardening and another who knew an unusual amount about sheep husbandry. Though not as lovely as Mairi, both ladies were attractive and possessed respectable intelligence. They asked him about Scotland, and he replied in a general way. The food and wine were good, and so the evening went along as it tended to do.

All perfectly boring especially since he was clearly the center of all female attention. After all, he would become a duke one day, and so every lady made sure to catch his attention at some point. Only one was so insistent that he had to pull out his brogue just to fob her off. After all, if she couldn't understand him, she would eventually leave him alone, right?

Wrong.

She was just starting to lose interest when Mairi looked up from the opposite side of the room. They had withdrawn to the parlor after the meal and were conversing in small groups before the cards were set out.

"He's only doing that to test you," she said to the impertinent woman. "If you can't understand him here, then how will you survive in Scotland?"

"Oh, but I understand every word!" the girl lied.

"I did, too!" another said.

And then it became a contest to see who could understand his thickest brogue. They all failed, of course. He knew words that weren't spoken in England and several that shouldn't be said in polite company no matter who understood. Even Sadie and Iseabail didn't catch them all, but Mairi was used to coarse men's talk and shot him a look of haughty disdain.

She was right, and he bowed to her in apology. It didn't work. She turned her attention to the gentleman currently discussing the benefit of various libations as if it were the key to political power. Apparently, the leader of the Tories preferred a special brand of port. Naturally, that reminded him that he was supposed to help sell Liam's whisky. It was the excuse he'd created so that he could travel with Mairi. That hadn't worked, but he still owed Liam the attempt.

"The company tonight has been so fine," he said loudly, "I've decided to let you all share in a special gift."

All the ladies grew very excited at that, but he held up his hand.

"I've a warning. It's a gift shared among Scots, and it'll test your mettle for sure."

One and all laughed at that, but he waved to the butler the way a magician begins a magic trick. Fortunately, Parry was ready, and he brought out a bottle that Connall had retrieved that afternoon.

"It's a very special blend of Scot's whisky given to me by Miss Mairi's laird. He and I grew up together as boys, and his clan makes the finest whisky in the world. He gives me a single bottle every year at Christmas, and I've saved them faithfully for a good occasion.

"What an excellent idea," said the countess. "We will celebrate the beginning of the London Season with you. I'm quite excited to get a sip."

"Only a sip, my lady," said Connall. "Scot's whisky is not for the faint at heart."

The butler poured everyone a glass, including the ladies, though their portions were much smaller. Mairi waved for a full measure, as did Sadie, but Iseabail declined with a laugh.

"I'm Scottish through and through," she said. "I don't need to prove it with a drink."

After a toast to everyone's health, they all drank. It was a good burn down his throat, and the warmth in his belly grew as he watched the men appreciate the drink. Enough, it seemed, that he would have sales for Liam by morning.

What surprised him, though, was the way Mairi downed her glass. He'd seen her drink over the years, but she never overindulged. She was prone to a ladylike sip or two before disappearing to handle her other duties. As the MacCleal chatelaine, she always had some task or another. And probably more significant, it always fell to her to deal with the drunks.

But tonight, she downed her drink like the burliest Scot and even called for a second while her cheeks turned bright red and her eyes grew wild. He didn't think the others noticed, but he had known Mairi for a very long time and he could see an edge of desperation in her that he didn't like.

If only she would talk to him, but she was a woman with more pride than sense. At least when it came to him, and so he stayed away. But he was getting tired of looking away from her when she was the only one in the room who interested him.

Sheep husbandry and gardening were valuable skills, ones that might help him once wed. But he looked for more in a wife, and these ladies acted like greedy innkeepers around him. They were desperate to please as they offered themselves for his perusal.

He found the whole thing distasteful and had no stomach for further conversation. Which meant he settled in the corner with a couple of the more genial gentlemen and together, they finished off the bottle. Fortunately for his limited supply of whisky, the party began to break up before he was tempted to open another bottle. And his drinking companions gave him coin for a case of whisky each, which would make Liam happy.

As each person said their good-byes, Connall remained gracious with the ladies and friendly with the gentlemen. Until finally—blessedly—the evening was done. At least for him and the countess. She bid everyone goodnight and disappeared upstairs. Sadie and Iseabail left as well, whispering to each other as they went. He made to seek his own bed until he realized that Mairi had not disappeared to her room. No, she'd gone to the kitchen, no doubt to help the staff with clean up. Or at least supervise.

That woman didn't know how to rest. Good thing he knew how to wait.

He heard her giving orders to Parry. She kept a kind tone as she questioned him, and then praised him and the other servants for a job well done. She ordered them to leave the rest for morning and seek their beds. He remained in the dark, nursing the last of the whisky, knowing she would come here soon enough. He heard the noise as the last servants went to bed, and then the soft whisper of her sigh as she climbed the stairs into the main hall.

He caught her then, stepping out of the shadows to blow out her candle. Then before he got a fist in the gut for his troubles, he spoke in a low voice.

"It's me," he said. "You're safe. But I've a mind to step outside for a bit and look at the stars. Thought you might be interested in joining me."

"It's not proper," she said.

"You've looked at the stars a thousand times alone or with others. None said a thing."

"Plenty said things, but no one heeded because they knew me better than that."

He let the silence hang for a moment, wrapping them in an intimacy that had his organ thickening despite his intention. Then he finally spoke. "I've a need to speak with you, Mairi. Will you no' give me a moment of yer time?" He let his brogue thicken and saw her shoulders ease a measure from the sound. He well remembered how hard it was to understand the Sassenach when he first went to school. The sound of a brogue felt good to him then well beyond the normal measure. He could see that it did the same for her.

"A moment only, Connall Aberbeag. And if you do anything I don't want—"

"You'll cut me to the quick one way or another."

"Do not doubt it."

He didn't. But rather than speak, he set his hand to her back and guided her down the kitchen stairs. There was a servant's entrance that led into an alley. A short walk landed them in a small bit of green in the vast brick of London. They travelled in silence, neither needing a coat. By the time they were in the small park, she was looking up at the sky with disgust.

"Not a star to be seen through all the coal dust."

"Nae, there's one." He stepped close to her and pointed up at the sky.

"One," she said, clearly grumbling about it. "And maybe a couple more, there and there."

"Aye." He sighed. "It's not like home, is it?" At home, he could see the vast array of the heavens. Here there was little but gray.

"Did you hear Mr. Berry complain about the cold? As if this is anything but a cool summer's night."

"Miss Gray and Miss Doyle agreed with him. Said they'd be shivering beneath their coats soon."

Mairi snorted. "Those two would agree with anything a man said, even if he claimed the sun was blue."

That was likely true. "Do they think a man is so weak that he must be complimented at every turn?"

She shrugged. "It would work with many a man, I suppose."

"I cannot imagine you doing something so silly."

"I don't know," she said, her tone becoming bitter. "I've flattered many a man just to get him to agree with what I wanted. It's the only way to handle a drunk."

He couldn't argue with her there, but he disliked thinking she ever had to manage with such men. He knew it had been part of her regular duties as the MacCleal chatelaine, but he thought that was wrong of the MacCleal. A woman should not be left alone to manage men. It was too dangerous, though obviously Mairi appeared to have held her own.

Which naturally brought to mind what he wanted to discuss with her. Still, it was an awkward transition to make. He did not like comparing his youthful follies to drunken men, but he couldn't deny the comparison. Just as they were overcome with drink, he'd been overwhelmed by his lust, and that was a shameful thing.

"Mairi," he said, his tone grave. "Seems to me we've got something between us that needs to be settled."

"No, Connall, we don't." Was there a hint of panic in her voice? He couldn't tell, but he couldn't go softer even if she was afraid of this conversation.

"But I think we do. Ten years ago, I was a brute with you. I wanted you so bad that I—"

"You've apologized before for this, Connall."

"I have. But you've never forgiven me for it, and I want to know why."

She sniffed as she turned away from him. "It's not for me to explain myself to you. There's no law that says I must forgive a man merely for saying sorry. The word's easy enough—"

"Have I ever done such a thing to you again?"

"You know better."

He did. "Have you heard tell of me doing anything akin to that again? With any lass?"

"They fall for you easy eno'. No need to take what's given willingly." Her brogue was getting stronger as her irritation grew.

"I've been turned down plenty, Mairi. I lost more than my control that day. I lost my best friend, and I want to know what it'll take to bring her back."

She jolted at his words, turning to face him with confusion on her face. The night was clear enough for him to see her. There might not be many stars, but the moon was bright enough.

"I was never your best friend, Connall Aberbeag. You've got men aplenty around you. And Liam—"

"Liam had his nose in a book most times. And you know that there's a distance between a laird's son and the rest of the clan. You were the one who could run as fast as I. You were one I told when my mother grew sick. And you were the one who held my hand when we laid her in the ground."

"That was a different time," she said, her voice gentle.

"Aye. It was a time I could still turn to you. I could speak my mind and have you understand. And when neither of us spoke, there was still a peace between us."

He saw her mouth open as if to speak, and he longed to hear what she would say. But in the end, her lips closed again. She looked over his shoulder, back toward the house, and he reached out to stop her from running. He didn't touch her, but she flinched as if he had. And that devastated him more than a scream.

"What have I done to make you fear me so?"

"You tease and you push, Connall Aberbeag, and you never stop."

"I spent a year letting you be back then. And when I heard nothing, I tried again the next spring. There've been months when you've not heard a peep from me and times when I bring you apples to have you throw them back in my face."

"You came to claim me like a sack of meal bartered for apples."

"I did not. I've brought you chocolate from Edinburgh and silk for a dress. I've spent more on you than I did my own mother."

"You hadn't any coin when your mother lived."

"And I've got better things to spend my money on than a woman who won't forgive."

She threw up her hands. "I forgive you! I forgave you within an hour of me crushing yer balls with my knee. An' so I've told you every time you think to bring this up again."

"Then why can't you look at me? Why do we pick at one another and make wagers on who will marry first?"

"Isn't that a friendship? I don't make wagers on my wedding with anyone else!"

He had no answer for her, no words to ask his question so she could answer plain. There was a distance between them beginning from that day. He longed to cross it, but he didn't know how.

"I'm about to pick a Sassenach to wed," he said. "And you as well. That will change both our lives, but I want to keep something of our old still. Something between us that could be good for both of us."

"You frighten me," she whispered.

Her words were so quiet that he nearly didn't catch them. But he had been studying her face and so read the words off her lips.

"I'd never hurt you."

She shook her head. "You don't even know what you do," she said. "When you're close to me, when I look at you..." She pressed her lips together.

"What?" She was so God-damned frustrating! Why wouldn't she finish her thoughts?

She lifted her chin such that her nose was tipped with silver. It was her fighting stance, but her words made no sense to him.

"I lose my thoughts!"

She glared at him as if that made sense.

"What thoughts?"

"My thoughts! My lists of things to do, the plans to be made, the work to be done, the reasons to—"

She did it again. She stopped her mouth as if... as if...

"The reasons to not kiss me, is it? You stay angry with me because you want to tumble into my arms?"

"Of all the arrogant, puffed-up conceit! You think I can't keep myself from kissing you?"

"You can't," he said, his thoughts tumbling back to the time in his bedroom. He'd been gentle with her, given her all the time in the world to run, and she hadn't. Sure, after he'd had a thorough taste of her, she'd broken away as if scalded. But there'd been plenty of ways to break long before their lips touched.

"Of course, I can!" She was all but screaming now. Her hands were fisted and her expression hot. But he also saw the way her breath was short and her nipples tight. Smart little buds pushed through the thin fabric of her gown.

"It's not me that frightens you," he said, realization dawning. "It's how you feel when I kiss you."

She shook her head. Indeed, the gesture was so tight and fierce, he wondered that it didn't give her a headache. But she didn't speak her denial. And if those pert nipples meant anything, she wanted his kiss for sure.

But he knew better than to take what she hadn't expressly given. That had been his mistake when he was a teen. So he tried a different approach.

"The feelings inside aren't bad, Mairi. They're the best thing ever."

"A full belly is best. A warm fire is best. A kiss is nothing—"

"It's not the kiss," he reminded her. "It's how you feel when we do it."

"It's not that pleasurable!"

"Isn't it no'?" he said. He took a step forward, and she retreated quickly. But there was little room in this small patch of green and she came up against a tree trunk after another step.

"Don't you dare touch me, Connall Aberbeag. I'll scream if you do."

He held up his hands, palms out. "I'll not do a thing until you ask."

She nodded, clearly reassured. Her arms were held tight to her sides and her fists were at the ready. She meant to punch him, it appeared. But only if he advanced, and he remained very still, two steps back from her. But he could still speak to her, couldn't he? And maybe his words would reach her.

"You've always been honest, Mairi, with yourself as well as everyone else. Tell me true, do you really think I'd hurt you? I'd do anything against your will?"

It took her a moment to answer, but in the end, honesty won out. "You haven't hurt me. You cannae."

Guilt rolled off his shoulders. All this time, he'd thought he'd hurt her beyond apology, beyond redemption. Now he saw that it wasn't him at all.

"So it's yourself you fear. You lose your tasks and your plans."

She looked away. He knew that she could still see him in the periphery, but her head was now canted away enough that her hair slipped past her cheek to cover half her face. His fingers itched to brush the lock aside. Indeed, the need to touch her burned through his blood, but he held himself back.

"Mairi," he said softly. "Can it be passion that frightens you?" It made sense. She'd always felt things keenly. It had taken her months to learn to skin a creature, not because she hadn't the skill with a knife or the hunger in her belly, but because she could not stop crying over the creature's death. That's why he'd turned to her when his mother died. He knew she felt the pain as keenly as he, though it was not her parent they buried.

"I had a plan, Connall."

"To marry Liam."

"We were promised when we were children. You know that."

"And I know he married someone else."

"Aye."

"Aye. So now you come down to London. Why? To marry another man who doesn't stir your loins?"

Her head snapped up. "You leave my loins out of it!"

He nearly laughed at that, but she would not take kindly to his humor. Fortunately, she wasn't so furious that she didn't hear the ridiculousness of her own words.

"You know what I mean," she said.

"I do. It means you're afraid of the tight nubs on your breasts. It means you are afraid of the wetness between your thighs and the heat in your belly. It means you touch your lips to remember my kiss, but then cut at me so you won't be tempted to feel my mouth on you again. It means, Mairi MacAdaidh, that you can't control yourself when I touch you and of all things, you like to be in control."

"You're daft," she snapped. "I don't control anything. If I could, I would have sent the MacCleal laird and his men away long before Liam came back with his wife. I wouldn't have seen my mother die nor yours either. I would set my father to smiling again, but he still cries at night when he drinks too much whisky. And that's nothing compared to the women I've seen die in childbirth, the babes who passed when they couldn't suckle, or the men out of their minds with fever from infection. I cared for the MacCleal clan when the laird was too drunk and Liam was in England with his books. If I had control, do you think my home would have been what it was?"

"No," he agreed. "But those are things only God controls, and if it were in any soul's hands, it would be yours. You've done all that and more when you were barely tall enough to stir the laundry. So you try to control what you can, and that's your thoughts, your hands, and your heart."

He saw a single tear slide down her cheek. She hastily brushed it away.

"It's not a failing, Mairi. No woman can control those things."

"And no man either!" she said. "So here we are, two creatures who cannae control themselves, and where will that lead? My parents were such, and I was born seven months after their wedding."

"They loved each other."

"She died while birthing my brother, and my father's never smiled so bright again."

"It doesn't have to be that way."

"Truly? What family do you know that hasn't felt pain, what grandparent who hasn't seen brother or mother or child die?"

"Grief comes to all in one form or another." This time he did touch her. He raised his hand ever so slowly to touch the back of her hand. He knew she saw it and was grateful she didn't pull away. "Denying what we feel makes no difference. It just makes us lonely."

She lifted her gaze to his. He saw the sheen of her tears and felt the rigidness in her body. She didn't disagree with him, but she wasn't going to give him an inch.

"It makes *you* lonely, Connall. It makes *me* safe."

And with that she jerked away from him. She headed back to the house with firm, heavy steps. He matched her easily, walking beside her while struggling for something to say. The words didn't come. When they finally made it back to the house and up the stairs, he tried to say more to her before her bedroom door. He opened his mouth to speak, but she shook her head.

Still he tried to shape words, but she stopped him with one of her own.

"No."

She didn't shout it, but it had the force of a blow. And then she went into her bedroom while he stood in the hall and tried to understand. How was it that he finally cleared himself of a guilt he'd been carrying for nearly a decade, and yet now he felt a thousand times worse than before?

CHAPTER THIRTEEN

MAIRI CLOSED THE door on Connall, then pressed her ear to the door. She wanted to know he walked away. Instead, she heard his sigh. It was a sound filled with frustration and disappointment. She'd heard it from him more and more as they'd grown up, and she knew it was her own contradictory actions that caused it.

Connall had the best laugh in the world, but she caused him to sigh, and that thought cut her deeply. He had been her best friend growing up. Now he was infected with the frustration she caused all her friends. That would be bad enough to spoil her night, but the worst was how angry she was with herself. Why couldn't she let herself go to Connall? She'd be a duchess. Her life would be secure and there'd be no worry about her losing her dowry. He had plenty of money.

But she couldn't do it. The fear was too strong in her to say something she knew terrified her. Everyone thought her fearless. She certainly gave that impression. But that was because she avoided the thing that truly terrified her: extreme feelings.

What had destroyed Scotland? The Jacobites' extreme worship of Bonnie Prince Charlie. What difference would one king or another make over their lives? Very little, and yet her own clan ended at Culloden, as did so many others. Those men were needed at home tending the crops and repairing their homes, but they'd left their families to die beneath a tide of bellowing anger and swords that did nothing against cannonballs.

Idiots.

But they were not alone in folly. She'd seen boys tempt fate and lose too many times. As a teenager, Connall was one of them, always testing his mettle against every other boy. Who could run faster, who could punch harder, who could throw, jump, or swim best? He'd beat them all eventually, but she'd learned her nursing skills tending his wounds and others. One boy had died from a fever contracted while swimming in a frigid stream. Another had broken his jaw in a fall and could not eat meat. It set wrong, and he grew sickly. In the end, winter ended what had begun that spring.

Just because Connall was the best of them didn't make him any less a fool. Adulthood had tempered his risky behavior. He no longer did a thing just because someone challenged him. But the temptation was still there, that devil-may-care attitude always ended with someone crying. She'd not be the one left with babes to feed while he was six feet under because of his own stupidity.

And then there was her own father. She'd been reared on tales of the great love between him and her mother. Passion had gripped them so much that they didn't wait to consummate their love until after the wedding. Mairi was born seven months into their marriage, not a respectable nine. Then that same hot passion had made her mother pregnant again too soon. According to the midwife who had been there, her mother was too weak to carry another child so soon after Mairi's birth. When she and the babe died, that selfsame passion broke her father. Many a night she'd caught him crying into his whisky over his lost love. And he had tears in his eyes whenever he remarked how much she looked like her mother.

The Scots were prone to wild emotions, brutal swings of temper, and fierce passion in love and hate. Which is why she would marry a Sassenach. She would find a quiet man—a boring one—and she would live her life away from the tears that flooded Scotland.

The maid had waited up to help her undress. She accepted her help, then sent the girl to bed. She doused the light and climbed into bed, but tired as she was, sleep eluded her. Her mind was filled with thoughts of Connall. She remembered that afternoon so long ago, the time he thought he'd ended their friendship.

They were both teenagers. He'd filled out in the last few years until he was a sight to behold. She found herself looking at his body in a new way. At the hair that sprouted on his chest and the sparkle in his eyes whenever she caught him looking at her curves. She'd gotten breasts that winter, and they weren't small ones. Connall liked to watch her play jumping games because of how they moved on her body. And she liked the way he looked at her, joy mixed with hunger.

She'd felt the passion stir then, but plenty of women had told her to beware. She didn't need the reminder. She'd helped the midwife through the winter and still heard the screams of women in labor. Most survived, of course, but the pain and the blood still frightened her. Her mother had died like that, in wrenching agony, and she had no wish to do the same herself.

And yet Connall watched her, and she always found a way to jump or dance or sashay whenever he was around. She was as much to blame for that day as he was.

She'd been sent to gather berries for the festival the next day, and he had come early with his father's men. Festivals were always busy with something happening everywhere and no one looking where two teenagers had gone, she to find berries, he to find her.

He surprised her when he popped up in the woods, but not too much. After all, he knew the land around her home nearly as well as she did. And he knew she would be picking berries because she made it a point to dawdle over the task when her friends were near. But this time Liam was away at school and the other girls were given different tasks. Connall had no doubt told his friends to go a different way because when he caught her about the waist, he whispered in her ear.

"We're alone," he said, "on a fine afternoon. Whatever shall we do?"

"I am picking blackberries," she said, holding up her basket and her stained fingers. "I don't care what you do."

He caught her hand and made a show of licking at the sweet stains. She remembered how his tongue had wrapped around and between her fingers. How her breasts had grown heavy and her belly moist. She knew when the wetness flowed between her thighs, and all because Connall Aberbeag sucked on her finger.

Her mouth had gone dry as she brushed her finger along the inside of his lower lip. She knew about a man's lust—at least in theory—and noticed too when his kilt lifted because of her.

It was the power of it all, she thought now, as she nibbled at her own fingertip. Connall was the most powerful boy in Scotland. The strongest, the boldest, the richest, and the most handsome. And yet there he was, lusting after her. She told him to carry her basket, and he did it. She told him to stand absolutely still, and he did so. Then she fed him a blackberry and let him lick not only her fingers, but the palm of her hand as well.

Her hands weren't idle either. She gripped his upper arm, loving the size and strength of him. His body was warm and alive, and he grinned when she squeezed.

"I think I'll pluck a berry for you," he said, and he did something she'd never forget. He pinched her left nipple through her blouse. It was summer and she'd ignored her stays, especially since she knew she'd be climbing and crawling through the brambles. So his hand was quick and the pinch sent a shock of feeling through her whole body.

She gasped when he did it then, and her breath caught now as she did the same in her bed. At the time, she'd stood frozen, surprise and delight keeping her in place. And then the cocky bastard had grinned and took that as permission to flatten his large hand over her breasts. He'd kneaded her tender chest, first with one hand and then both.

What sensations! She'd been hard put to stay standing as he moved his hands clumsily over her.

She was more careful now, knowing exactly what to do when her hands touched her breasts. Back then, he'd caught her up in his arms and carried her to a soft pile of grass. He lay her down, and she'd let him open her blouse such that her breasts were touched by the sun and the breeze. Nothing felt as good as his mouth on her nipples.

She used her fingers now to mimic what he'd done. She pulled at her nipples just as he'd sucked them. She pinched as he'd nipped. And her belly rippled while her breath caught. He hadn't been patient then. Big and clumsy as he pressed her down, but she hadn't cared. He didn't force himself on her. It was just his mouth on her breast and her undulating on the grass in time with what he did.

Then he raised his head with such a grin.

"Lass," he whispered, and she'd frowned at him. She wasn't any "lass." She was herself and had no desire to become one of those girls talked about by the boys working glass furnace. She knew what the men said, and the idea that he thought her like one of them soured her.

But she hadn't time to express it. Instead, he'd kissed her roughly. His mouth had come hard down on hers and he'd stuck his tongue in when she cried out. That had been the turning point in their encounter. Her emotions had cooled enough with his awkward kiss that she shoved him back. And when he rocked back on his heels, she scrambled backwards.

"Lass?" he'd said. Not her name. Not, "What's the matter?" Just a dazed word that could apply to any girl, and a cock so big it thrust up his kilt like a thick stick.

It was awful, and yet her heart had been beating, her breasts were still tender, and part of her wanted him to go back to them. Tease her nipples again, and her legs would spread. She was sure of it because she'd already started.

And damn her for still wanting it now. For looking at the

thrust of his cock then and wanting to see it revealed.

"No!" she'd bellowed. The word was meant for herself. It was defiance against the emotions that seemed to tear through her. She wanted him, and she did not. She wanted those feelings, and she did not. She wanted to know, and she already did. Hadn't she seen women screaming in childbirth? Wasn't that enough to tell her to flee?

It was then. She'd run like the wind, the blackberries forgotten. He'd followed sometime later. She knew because he'd filled up her basket with blackberries and brought them to the kitchen. She'd spent the rest of the day and the next by the glass furnace using heat and sweat to keep her feelings at bay. And she'd always worn her stays after that.

Sometime in the decade since that disaster, Connall had learned how to kiss. And damn him for that because his terrible kiss had been the only thing that saved her last time. But now, lying in the dark of her bedroom, she relived every slow caress of his mouth on hers. The way he'd made her lips tingle and how he'd stroked against her teeth until she'd opened for him. In her imagination, he thrust and parried with her tongue, and her breath grew short again, her body boneless.

Lying in her bed, her hands stroked her breasts and down by her sides. He'd never done this in reality, but in her imagination, they'd done what all passionate Scots do. They'd gotten carried away and damn the consequences. She could do that in the privacy of her own bed. Here, she could feel everything and never fear that feelings would tear her apart.

She touched herself between her thighs where she was slick and open. She thrust her fingers inside and pretended it was Connall's cock, thick and hard. She beat a tempo there and rolled her thumb over her nub. In her mind's eye, it was Connall on top of her pressing her hard into the mattress. Connall inside her, ramming her with powerful thrusts. Connall lost in his need for her while she tightened around him.

Her abdomen tensed and her breasts jerked with her breath.

She knew better than to cry out, but she heard the rasp of her need. And then she thought of him everywhere at once. Cock pounding inside her. Hands on her breasts. Tongue in her mouth.

He filled her and consumed her. And she rode him as she might a stallion, straight to her peak.

She came with a muted cry then flopped back on the bed as she bonelessly rode the waves of fulfillment. And in her mind's eye, Connall gathered her to him, curled against her back, and together they slept in perfect, peaceful contentment.

She could do that because none of it was real. Whatever emotions possessed her now, they could be safely put away by morning.

CHAPTER FOURTEEN

T HE SEASON BEGAN in earnest after that, and Connall found his time filled with nonsense. He was a man used to working his lands, managing the disputes between his clansmen, and negotiating trades with his neighbors. Now he was strolling through Hyde Park, attending musical evenings, and dancing at Almack's.

That would have been pleasant enough if it weren't for the scores of women constantly begging for his attention. It was his title they were after. Every female gushed over him before he'd done anything but acknowledge them with a nod. He found himself becoming more reserved by the second. Hard to say anything when the smallest statement was greeted with, "What a clever thing to say! I'm astounded by your perception!" Even the gentlemen acted this way, and he began to long for an insult or cutting word.

Thankfully, Mairi was always nearby to burst the bubble of overdone fawning. When one woman went on about the gloriousness of his hair, Mairi casually mentioned that he used a setting potion made from the blood of lambs. "It's the best for getting curls to lay just right," she said. And she didn't stop there. She made up a recipe for the concoction on the spot and the woman wrote it down, swearing she would try it as soon as possible.

That same day, a gentleman complimented him on the

breadth of his shoulders, the narrowness of his waist, and the strength in his calves. Mairi sauntered over to explain that it was because of Scottish hay. She claimed that the Aberbeag laird insisted that all his children eat hay every morning with whisky and that was why Connall was so handsome a specimen.

Her comments grew more outlandish every day. It became a game of hers to see what the Sassenach would believe. And it was his game to see if he could make her laugh as he agreed with every wild thing she said. It was the baby bathing in beet juice that finally broke her reserve. She said it created a reddish character (whatever that meant) and he agreed it was important to counter the MacAdaidh yellow tendency caused by witch hazel. A yellow character, he explained, held too much sunshine in it and needs must be softened to the color of a dawn by beet-bathing the babies soon after birth.

The tongue twister was what finally broke through her facade. They were walking in a group in Hyde Park and Mairi gurgled as she tried to stifle her laughter. It didn't work. She had to hide behind her fan as she guffawed in a most unladylike manner. It was the first genuine expression he'd seen on her face in a week, and he couldn't be more pleased.

The gentleman she was with was horribly offended, and he sniffed at the insult before turning away to talk to another lady who had joined their party. Connall didn't mind. The man was a puffed-up prig. Connall also didn't care that they'd insulted the seventeen-year-old girl who'd been attached to his side like a leech the moment they'd arrived in Hyde Park.

He hoped she and the prig would have a lovely conversation together. Or whoever was around them. Goodness, they'd grown to a group of a dozen as they strolled through the park at the fashionable hour. But by a stroke of luck, he had a chance for semi-private conversation with Mairi.

"Is something amiss?" he asked, sotto voce.

She glanced up, the mirth dying to her customary grimness. "You can ask me that when you just made me laugh like a braying goat?"

"Not that. I've never seen you so determined before. Not even when you are shaping glass. At Almack's you looked downright fierce."

"At Almack's I was admonished for being Scottish, told to smile brighter, step lighter, darken my expression, and to stop walking on my toes. And that was all in the first fifteen minutes."

Yes, he had heard some of the criticisms. Every adult woman at Almack's felt like it was appropriate to give advice to the debutantes, and much of it contradicted itself. "But what about the gentlemen?"

She snorted. "They were dim and smelled bad, but I preferred them to the ones who thought I would allow liberties just because I am—"

"Scottish." He said the word with her. Truthfully, he hadn't realized how much his own people despised the Sassenach until he began to hear it from the other side. What the English thought of the Scots was downright hideous, and no wonder their two people had trouble getting along. Bitter history aside—and many could not set it aside—but when a girl believed Scotsmen bathed their babies in beet juice, then there was a breakdown in communication somewhere.

"Has anyone hurt you?" he asked quietly.

She shot him a wry look. "Ask instead if I hurt any of them."

"I don't care if you did. If you give me their names—"

"No," she said firmly. "It's no more than any woman receives here or in Scotland. I learned how to twist a man's finger until it popped long before I grew old enough to understand why."

"I would that they treat you with respect," he snapped. "Everywhere in the world."

She smiled in genuine pleasure. "I've never felt threatened around the Aberbeag."

"If a man steps out of line, you tell me. Here or there, you tell me." He frowned. "You must signal me somehow."

She chuckled. "Am I to wave a flag at you? Would you see it

over the heads of all your admirers?"

Probably not. He'd thought the feather in her hair that first night was odd. He'd never realized how tasteful it was until he saw the myriad types of feathers, ribbons, and extreme creations that adorned everyone else's head. "Mairi," he sighed, "I fear I cannot breathe sometimes for all the females around me."

"It's marriage season. Didn't you expect it?"

"I did. But the experience of it…" He tried not to shudder.

"I was unprepared as well."

"Is that why you scowl at everyone?" He took her arm and slowed her steps. "Mairi, tell me true. What is the matter? We have been a week at this nonsense and today was the first time I saw you smile."

Her shoulder stiffened, and he released her. "Don't be silly," she said, her voice high and clearly false. "I smile all the time." Then to prove it, she flashed a brilliant look at a gentleman walking down a contrary path from them.

"I mean a true smile," he said, letting his brogue thicken. "If you think I cannae see the difference then you misjudge me."

She looked at him, and he watched as her expression shifted from defiant to tired. She was the fiercest woman he knew, but at the moment, she appeared to have aged a decade, and the sight horrified him.

"Mairi—" he began, but she cut him off.

"Connall, I do not like these men," she said in a harsh whisper. "The countess says they're the best that I can hope for with no dowry, but they're old or smelly or dumb."

"Then don't marry them," he said. "You have a home in Scotland, a father who cares for you, work with glass if not at the castle. You don't have to—"

"But I want to!" she hissed. "I want to marry and have children. I wasn't sure at first, but—"

"You've been listening to the countess." The woman practically worshiped the married state. She spoke gloriously of having children and pitied the poor unwed as if they were deficient somehow.

"Not the countess," she said. "Her daughters."

Ah. Each of the lady's children had found a mate that seemed to suit them. Though Amber and Sophie were increasing, they had still managed to visit this past week. And they all knew how blissfully happy Lilah was. She'd gotten married in Scotland. The only one yet to appear was Lady Gwen, but the tales of her "daffodil courtship" as it was now called, were a frequent topic of conversation. He had to admit that speaking with their husbands had left him with a deepening longing for the right wife. Like them, he wanted a woman who understood him. One he could share his life with. He had yet to imagine himself with any of the women he'd met so far.

"The Season has barely begun," he said. "There may yet be someone." It surprised him how hard it was to say those words. He hated the idea of her with any man except for himself. But she had made her decision clear. And if it could not be him, then he wanted her happy. And that meant she needed to wait for a man who suited her.

"I got another bill from the dressmaker's," she said. "The countess brought it to me today."

He nodded. He hadn't missed her statement that she had no dowry. After all her claims of saving for her future, he was surprised at her lack now. But he didn't ask her for fear of upsetting her pride.

"Do you have enough?" he asked.

"I do. But I... My dowry..." Her voice trailed away.

He took her hand and squeezed it as he set it on his arm. "Not every lady has money. Unlike them, you are brilliant, capable, and would make any man proud to have as a wife."

She nodded and he could see the effort it cost her to smile up at him. She was frightened about her future, and the difference between her now and the fiery woman he'd known all his life made him gnash his teeth. But what could he say? He had already offered himself and been refused.

Still, he wanted to try. He gripped her hand and pulled her closer to him, but they were in public and several young ladies thought he had been private with Mairi for too long. They hovered nearby and did their best to catch his attention. And while he was still searching for the right words for Mairi, three sisters with identical horse-like laughs surrounded them and demanded he give his opinion on their new dresses. He responded with a compliment, as usual. It was what they expected and the quickest way to dismiss them. But by the time he had finished with the sisters, Mairi had joined Sadie and Iseabail as they chatted with several young bucks.

To anyone else, the group appeared at ease, delighted by witty conversation on a brilliant autumn afternoon. To him, though, he saw Mairi's too bright smile and the way she seemed to hang on gentlemen's words even as she held herself apart from them.

She wanted to want them, but her body betrayed her. She had no more interest in the three handsome men than she did cleaning a stag brought in for a feast. She knew how to do it but took no pleasure in the process. And for that, his heart ached. The search for a husband should not be so painful. But what could he do to help her?

He had no answer during their promenade in Hyde Park. He was at a complete loss during the early musicale evening. It wasn't until the ball that night that he felt inspiration strike. Over the years he'd seen Mairi in several states. He'd seen her flushed with sweat as she worked glass, furious as she disciplined a lazy servant or harassed a drunk to bed, and once he'd seen her stumbling drunk during a festival when she was fifteen. In all of that, her body had moved with fluid grace.

Except now. She was dancing like a broken marionette, all stiff-armed and jerky. Her smile looked like it was painted on, her arms were alternately too rigid or too loose, and her feet never seemed to coincide with her balance. He thought at first that she was drunk, so uncoordinated were her movements. But when she turned and he looked at her face, he realized that she was on the verge of tears. Indeed, she was holding them back by sheer force of will.

What the hell had happened?

The sight of her was so shocking to him that he nearly broke through the dancers to grab her away. Instead, he held on to his temper and his worry and waited. Thankfully, the set ended quickly and there did not appear to be any man waiting for her hand in the next set.

He met her the moment she stepped off the dance floor, bowed over her hand, and pulled her away. She didn't even bother to bid her dance partner farewell, and that made him want to punch the bastard in the face.

"What did he do to you?" he asked, the words sounding very much like a growl.

"What? Nothing."

"Don't lie to me," he said as he pulled her into a dark alcove. It wasn't exactly private. They could be easily overheard, but it would do for the moment. "You look like you're going to be sick."

"I'm fine," she said, her tone weary.

"What did he say to you? Did he do something?"

"What? No!" She crossed her arms defensively. "He was perfectly fine. Boring, pads his clothing badly, but nothing unusual."

He shook his head. "Something happened. I can tell."

"You're imagining things."

He wasn't, but she wasn't going to talk with him growling at her. He softened his tone and his expression. He put away his need to punch someone for upsetting her. And he tried to be gentle with her though it was not at all how he was used to acting.

"You are pale and listless. You're moving like a broken puppet and your smile—"

"What about my smile?" she snapped as she flashed him a

hideous caricature of a smile. "Is it too bright? Too wide? Too toothy? Not enough purse to my lips? Or perhaps you'd like to criticize my dress? My hair? How I eat? How about my shoes?"

He reared back at her tart tone. Damn it, she was clearly in a temper and truthfully, he was glad of it. She'd shown more spirit in the last minute than she had during the whole last set.

"Mairi, what has happened?"

She threw up her hands in disgust. "What hasn't happened?" She sighed. "I'm not popular. Gentlemen aren't flocking to me. I'm mostly ignored or criticized at every turn. By everyone! My last partner told me my teeth were all wrong!"

"There's nothing wrong with your teeth." They were white, and she had all of them.

"And yet he felt compelled to tell me what was wrong with them."

"Then he's an idiot."

"Really?" she gasped in mock surprise. "I didn't realize that."

He winced. "I don't understand how that made you so upset." She shot him a hard look, and he hastily amended his words. "Upset enough to look like a—"

"A broken puppet. I heard you."

He sighed. "You are a beautiful woman with the grace of a stag."

"A what?" she gaped at him. "I'm large with antlers on my head?"

"That's not what I meant, and you know it."

"I don't know what you mean by dragging me off to the side and yelling at me."

If anyone was yelling, it was her. "There's a power in a stag that is undeniable. It's majestic, it holds its head high, it moves with power and speed."

"And would terrify these lily-livered Sassenach."

He tilted his head. Certainly, there were weak Englishmen, just as there were idiot Scotsmen. "You've met no man who can equal you?"

She sighed and leaned back against the wall. "None that want me. I thought they would see my worth. I thought someone would see me instead of my dress and my heritage."

He touched her upper arm. It was the only part of her arm not covered by a glove. "You haven't shown them who you are. You've been playing their game of prancing about and smiling too much—"

"Or too little. Or too wide—"

"Or with the wrong teeth. What do you care about any of that?"

She looked at him. "If I want a husband—"

"Then be yourself."

She sighed. "I have been and—"

"Not the angry Mairi. The strong one. The beautiful one. The one who wants to be here."

"At the ball?"

"The dance, the ball, the Marriage Mart. Be the woman who wants to live her life with a fierceness that defies everyone else and their stupid teeth. That woman is irresistible."

She had no real understanding of what he meant and no wonder. He could barely comprehend his own words. He knew only that she was not being the woman he adored. She'd hidden that person away, and it made him want to weep for missing her.

Or punch the stupid man who criticized her teeth. What an idiotic thing to say.

"Come dance with me. Show them the woman you are, teeth and all."

She shook her head. "The next one is a waltz, and you don't dance that."

He didn't, not because he couldn't but because the women put too much store in who partnered whom in a waltz. He'd met several interesting ladies this past week, but none that he wanted to encourage with a waltz.

Mairi was different.

He held out his hand. "I've seen you dance. You move like

the wind on a summer's day, like a—"

"Stag in heat?"

He growled at her, but it was a playful sound. "I am not good with words," he began.

"Actually," she said as she took his hand. "You're very good with them. And I thank you."

She was going to waltz with him? Excellent!

He led her onto the dance floor. He was aware that others were watching them, but he didn't care. She was in his arms and looking to him for help. He knew what to do. It was simply a matter of spinning her around so quickly that she laughed. And once she laughed, her body would relax, and she would be the woman she was meant to be. Bright, happy, and a diamond among paper doll women with no substance, no strength, and no brilliance.

The music began, and so did they. He was going to bring out the real Mairi if it took all night.

CHAPTER FIFTEEN

THIS WAS NOT a waltz. Mairi had danced the waltz before, moving in a three-step tempo about the ballroom. Her partners had been acceptable dancers, some led better than others, one had stepped on her toes, and another had pulled her too close so that she purposely stepped on his toes. In every case, she had smiled where was appropriate and done what was needed to make the event a pleasant activity.

Connall was not dancing a waltz. Despite the beat of the music, in defiance of the other people on the floor, Connall was doing something completely his own. He gripped one hand around her waist and the other raised her arm up high. Then he lifted and spun her around as if he were dancing with a doll. At first, she was shocked. Did he know that people were watching them? That they'd be shocked and appalled by the ridiculous Scots?

Then she was impressed. How strong was he that he could lift her off the floor like this? He swung her up so high that the air lifted her gown to a shocking degree. Then she would touch down enough to steady herself before he swung her around again. Whatever this was had her spending more time in the air than on the ground.

It was like being a child again, twirling around in her father's arms. Nothing could hurt her, and everything was new. How she laughed—then and now. The giggles burst from her, especially when she finally understood Connall's rhythm. Instead of being flung around like before, she timed her few steps with a jump that helped launch her into the air. What started as a startling display of strength became a delightful jump and soar dance.

How wonderful to feel the unrestrained joy of movement. She'd lost that, she realized. As she'd grown, every moment of her life had a purpose. All she did was work of one kind or another, even the work to find a husband. Especially the finding of a husband. When had she last run down a field because it was fun? Or spun in a circle until she was so dizzy she dropped to the ground?

Not since she was a child. Not until now when Connall helped her jump almost to the ceiling and then caught her as she came back down. And when he began to spin her around, she clutched him with both hands and grinned with him as the world became nothing but a blur.

All she saw was him. The way his eyes were alight with happiness. The way he grinned at her because she was grinning at him. And the way his neck and shoulders flexed with power as he lifted her. His arms were rock solid, and his balance was perfect.

And when he set her back on the earth, her world settled into a manageable place. She took a joyous breath perhaps for the first time in London.

"There she is," he said, his brogue thick. "Welcome to London, Mairi MacAdaidh. I've been waiting fer ye."

So had she. How had she lost that confidence for which she was so well known? The solid knowledge that whatever came, she would find a way through. Hard work didn't bother her. Disapproving stares never touched her. She did what was needed and beware to anyone who tried to stop her.

"You are a crazy Scotsman," she said, "to swing me like that at a London ball." Her tone was full of admiration. What man dared to do such a thing except Connall Aberbeag?

"I grew tired of waiting for your laugh."

She laughed then, the sound starting as a chuckle but growing to a guffaw that had tears streaming from her eyes. She tried to cover her mouth. Good lord, the English were staring at them as if they were crazy. And perhaps they were. At least *she* felt completely undone.

Then he gently pulled her hand away from her mouth and raised it up to his face. He kissed the back of her hand while his merry eyes stayed steady on her face. And when he straightened up, she dropped into the most proper curtsey a woman could ever do. She would give the king himself no more than what she gave to Connall.

And when she straightened, she smiled at him. "Thank you."

"My pleasure," he returned.

They held like that for a long moment. He didn't seem to want to break the connection of their gazes, and she couldn't have done it if she tried. He mesmerized her. But then, he blinked and turned to the ballroom at large.

"My apologies," he said. "It seems I was overcome with madness." He turned to the orchestra. "Please may we begin that waltz again? I shall try to keep my...um..."

"Scottishness?" Mairi offered in an undertone.

"Er, yes." He winked at her. "I shall keep my Scottishness under control this time."

A few people chuckled at that. Others merely scowled. But in the end, the orchestra began again. A proper waltz which they danced properly. In truth, they danced it beautifully.

Mairi trusted his strength and his balance, and with every step she allowed herself to relax a measure more. Soon they were whirling about the ballroom in a way that was every bit as much flight as her jumping, spinning experience from before. But this time she was less a child laughing in delight, and more a woman who matched her body to a man. Their steps were measured to one another, and they grew faster and more daring together.

She could not have done this with any other man. And when she looked in his eyes, she saw the same thought reflected there. He could not do this with any other woman.

There were more thoughts spinning at the edge of her awareness. Questions about what that might mean and what she should do next. But she didn't want to think about anything right then. She was too wrapped up in the experience of him holding her as they moved through the world. It was just a ballroom, and yet she felt it as if it were more. Perhaps if they stepped just right, if the fairies blessed them, and the weather held kind, then they could be like this forever. Completely in sync, completely at ease, no matter what else happened in the world.

Maybe.

Then the music ended. They slowed to a stop, but he didn't let her go and she couldn't look away.

"Mairi," he said, the word half plea, half groan.

She nodded. "Yes."

She wasn't sure what she meant by that. The word held acknowledgment and surrender. To what, she had no conscious idea. But she couldn't take back the promise once uttered. Time would show her what they'd just done. And she had faith that Connall would see her safely through it.

CHAPTER SIXTEEN

ISEABAIL WATCHED AS Connall waltzed Mairi about the room. Their display had been shocking to most, dismaying to her, and yet still unbelievably romantic. How was it that everyone else had all the luck in love while she struggled to find a man who might be slightly acceptable?

"What are you doing?" Sadie asked as she pinched Iseabail's arm above her glove.

"Ow! What are *you* doing?"

"I'm not staring like a lovelorn waif at the dance floor. Who were you supposed to dance with?"

She sighed, feeling the burn of disappointment in her gut. "Connall."

"Really? But he never promises waltzes."

She lifted her dance card where she'd purposely left this waltz blank. "He promised that if no one asked me, he'd dance with me."

Sadie shook her head. "You've been dancing every waltz. You're a titled lady with a dowry."

Iseabail nodded. "I held this one open for him."

"But why?" Sadie pointed at the dance floor. Connall had just spun Mairi around so fast that she laughed out loud. The countess would say they were making a spectacle of themselves, and they certainly were, but it was clear neither cared. Mairi finally showed signs of dropping her foul mood and Connall was grinning like it was Christmas morning. "He can't see anyone but her."

"I know," Iseabail said. Fear rose up higher in her throat for all that she tried to shove it down.

"There are other men you like. You told me so."

It was true. "Do you think any of them could face my uncle and win?"

She saw the answer on Sadie's face. None of these pampered Englishmen knew how to fight with anything other than words and most were not very good at that. They set dogs to chase foxes and called themselves hunters. Her uncle's men would make mincemeat of them.

"Come take a stroll with me," Sadie said with a smile that indicated mischief. "The countess is playing cards. We can wander outside."

By "wander outside," Sadie meant play games with the gentlemen who followed her. After a lifetime under her mother's vicious thumb, Sadie was taking risks that no proper girl should take. Where Iseabail studied every gentleman for a man who could protect her, Sadie was looking for fun, fun, fun. Just that. Entertainment without thought to the danger.

"You can't keep kissing men just because they ask," Iseabail said.

Sadie chuckled. "Some don't ask."

"Even worse!"

Rather than answer, her friend hooked arms with her and began walking them both toward the open doors. Tonight's ball was in Grosvenor Square in a home that boasted a garden off the ballroom. Several couples were already taking the air and Sadie laughed with delight when two gentlemen joined them.

The nearest one bowed to them. "Miss Allen, Honorable Iseabail." He winked when he used a version of Iseabail's full title, as if he were the only one who had ever done so. "Fancy meeting you here where we were told to be."

Iseabail gaped at her friend. "Sadie! Are you insane?"

"We're just taking a walk!" Sadie said as she held out her arm to the speaker. "Good evening, Mr. Carr. Shall we wander?"

"It would be my pleasure," the man responded as he grabbed hold of Sadie's arm. He appeared to know right where he wanted to take her. While Iseabail watched in dismay, the two headed down a path that would take them off the house grounds and into the dark neighborhood.

Meanwhile, the second gentleman was bowing low before her. "Mr. Preston Barrett, at your service."

Yes, she knew who he was. A second son who fancied himself a poet. He had no discernable skills beyond a very pretty face and a silver tongue. That might work in London, but it did her no good against her uncle. He was known to be in Mr. Carr's company often as they were neighbors, and Mr. Carr would one day be a baron.

"Good evening, Mr. Barrett. I wonder if we might..." She was about to say go back, but Sadie and her beau were already heading into the shadows. The girl had lost herself in a wild quest to have fun for the first time in her life. But Iseabail knew the folly of thinking oneself too strong to be overpowered. Sadie's gentleman might be narrow of stature, but he was still tall and might not want to stop after a few kisses. "Damnation," she cursed. "We need to go after them."

"Don't worry, my lady," Mr. Barrett said. "Eugene won't hurt her. Just wants a little nip and tickle, if you get my meaning."

She did. She also knew how a little bit could quickly turn into too much. "Let's find them," she said.

"Of course, though we don't have to be too fast at it, do we?" He stroked the inside of her arm. Truthfully, the caress felt nice, even through her glove. She wasn't immune to the pleasure of a man's touch. His stroke made her skin tingle, and he was pretty enough. She wouldn't mind kissing him, and indeed, why not? Just for a little bit. She could forget her fears if only for a moment.

She let him draw her deeper into the shadows. She wasn't exactly agreeing, but she wasn't disagreeing either. Perhaps if she knew more about him—

A screech cut through the air. It didn't sound like Sadie, but she couldn't be sure. Twisting out of Mr. Barrett's hold, she dashed into the darkness. Her hands were balled into fists, and she was ready to strike out, but what she saw had her slowing her steps.

Sadie's gentleman was on the ground, his hands shoved between his knees. Sadie stood above him, shaking her head.

"Tsk, tsk, Mr. Carr. When a lady says no, she means no."

The man looked up at her and started cursing her in terms that were rather mundane despite the vehemence with which he spoke. The words were crude and vicious, but rather common. Meanwhile, Mr. Barrett appeared to be very uncomfortable.

"I say, Gene, that's not very nice." He stepped forward and held out his hand. "Get up now. You're ruining your coat."

His cousin grabbed his wrist and slowly hauled himself upright. His face was a mottled red and he remained hunched over his balls, but there was venom in his eyes when he looked at Sadie.

"You Scottish bitch!" he hissed.

Sadie watched him with an amused expression as she smoothed down her skirt. She opened her mouth to say something impertinent. Sadie did love being impertinent, but she never got the chance.

While Iseabail was wondering if anyone else had heard Mr. Carr's squeal, the man abruptly lunged for Sadie. He caught everyone by surprise, Sadie included. She slammed backwards into a tree, grunting at the impact. Mr. Carr raised his fist, ready to strike, but Iseabail got there first. She rabbit-punched the bastard as quick as she could right in his side.

It distracted him, but it didn't cause much damage. She didn't have enough power in her punches to stop a man deep in his fury. Mr. Carr rounded on her, and she scrambled backwards. She stumbled over Mr. Barrett who was doing nothing but standing there gaping, and her footing got fouled in his big feet.

She stumbled and fell backwards onto her rump. Mr. Barrett

squeaked in alarm and jumped in the opposite direction. Iseabail looked up in dismay, seeing the raw emotion in Mr. Carr's face. She'd seen the same naked fury on other men. She knew how dangerous it was.

She tried to gain her feet, but she was in a gown on the ground. Her slippers gave no traction and—

A branch came down hard on Mr. Carr's temple. A single whack that dropped him where he stood. Sadie had power in her swing, and that branch was thick and heavy, so the sound of impact had been gruesome indeed. Fortunately, it still did its job. Mr. Carr crumpled until he dropped face-first onto the ground. Then he lay there, preternaturally still, while Sadie tossed the branch aside.

"Damn," she cursed. "That was a better blow than I expected."

"Did he hurt you?" Iseabail gasped.

"Me? No. What about you?"

"I'm fine," she said as she finally gained her feet. Her dress might be stained, but given that the ground was dry, perhaps there hadn't been much damage.

"I knocked him out," Sadie said, disgust filling her tone.

"Why do you sound upset by that?"

"Because I wanted to tell him something."

"What could you possibly need to say to him?"

Sadie shrugged, then turned her gaze to poor Mr. Barrett who had a handkerchief pressed to his face. He was sweating profusely and looking like a trapped rabbit.

"I guess you'll just have to tell him," Sadie said.

"What?" The word came out in another squeak. Honestly, didn't Englishmen's voices ever drop?

"We know about you now," Sadie said as she brushed a bit of bark off her hands. "We know what you did to Miss Duncan."

"I didn't do a thing!" Mr. Barrett said, his voice still painfully high.

Iseabail snorted. "Just a nip and tickle?"

Sadie shook her head. "He wanted a great deal more than that, and you, Mr. Barrett, helped him. You're the well-spoken one. He's the rapist."

Oh God. Now she remembered the story Sadie had whispered to her one night last week about one of their fellow debutantes who had been accosted. "Miss Duncan?" she asked, finally understanding that Sadie had been avenging an abused woman.

Sadie glanced at Iseabail. "She's fine, thank God. A maid interrupted him and helped her." She squatted down and deftly felt through Mr. Carr's pockets. "But he broke her necklace and now she's terrified that all men are like him."

They might very well be.

Sadie held up a fat purse. "Excellent."

Mr. Barrett cried out. "That's robbery!"

"Actually, it's recompense for the necklace and gratitude to the maid." Sadie straightened up. "Now here's my message, Mr. Barrett." Her tone was ice cold. "We know about you and him now, and we're telling everyone who might not know. *Everyone.* That means you're no longer accepted in polite society. No woman will have you. No hostess will allow you in her doors."

"But I didn't do anything!" the man whined.

Iseabail looked at him in disgust. "Exactly. You didn't stop him and that's enough."

"But that's not fair!" he cried, as if he'd never learned that life wasn't fair.

Meanwhile, Sadie pocketed the purse and linked arms with Iseabail. "Let's go back inside. I'm feeling in the mood to dance."

Iseabail laughed. How could she not? The girl had just knocked out her attacker and was practically singing with glee. With an airy wave, the two of them left the men to stroll quickly back to the ball.

"You planned for this," Iseabail accused in a low tone. "You went with him on purpose!"

"Of course, I did. Do you really think I'd risk my reputation with a blighter like that?"

Iseabail had thought so. Apparently, she'd been wrong. "But you could have been seriously hurt."

"Not me. Miss Duncan was pretty banged up. No one teaches these English girls how to punch." She tapped her side where Mr. Carr's coins clinked loudly. "But this will cheer her up."

"You cannot do that again, Sadie."

"Don't plan to."

"And if you do, then you must warn me. I could have been more help—"

"But you're a terrible actress, Iseabail. And you would have hovered. It was best done this way." They were back in the correct garden now and the lantern light illuminated them both. "Turn around," Sadie ordered. "Let me see if your dress is ruined."

Iseabail turned and heard Sadie's grunt of dismay.

"Is my dress torn?" she asked, trying to look at her own behind.

Sadie shrugged. "We'll need to leave. I just need to tell Miss Duncan's grandmother what happened. She'll make sure our reputations remain pure."

"You told her grandmother and not me?" Iseabail huffed.

"You're a terrible actress, remember?"

"I'm terribly cross with you, too," she said, though there was no heat in her words. In truth, she was impressed by Sadie's bravery. Iseabail had done some desperate things in her life, not the least of which was running across half of Scotland to find Sadie. But she'd done them because she'd had no choice. Sadie, on the other hand, had done something dangerous out of the goodness of her heart. That set her head and shoulders above anyone Iseabail knew.

Meanwhile, Sadie looked back one last time. "You don't think I killed him, do you?"

A shudder went through Iseabail at the idea. Though she wasn't sure if she felt safer with the man dead or alive. "I don't think so, but blows to the head can be tricky."

"Well, he deserved it—"

"Most definitely!"

"And Mr. Barrett will be able to help him. Or not. Honestly, I don't care."

On that, they agreed. Soon they were inside the ballroom where they headed directly to the cluster of older women. Widows, grandmothers, and chaperones sat on the edge of the dance floor, and they all looked up as Sadie approached.

There was approval all around as Sadie spoke with Miss Duncan's grandmother and passed over the purse. Somehow the countess became aware of their activities and bustled over with a very tight expression. She seemed horribly upset by it all and worried about the consequences to their reputation. Fortunately, Miss Duncan's grandmother was there to reassure them. Apparently, the grandmothers and chaperones had already been whispering about Mr. Carr and Mr. Barrett. Now, thanks to Sadie's bravery, the women of the *ton* could align against those two horrible men. Neither Sadie's nor Iseabail's marital prospects would be harmed from tonight's antics, but they were admonished to never, ever do something like this again.

Iseabail agreed with alacrity, as did Sadie. Iseabail was being honest. She wasn't so sure about Sadie. In either event, it wasn't until hours later when she was in bed and had finally stopped whispering with Sadie that Iseabail had a shocking thought.

She realized that she hadn't thought about Connall for hours now. And surprisingly, that didn't bother her one bit.

CHAPTER SEVENTEEN

F OR MAIRI, THE trip home from the ball was bizarre. She had no idea why the countess called for their wraps and the carriage while Mairi and Connall were dancing the next set with new partners. Indeed, the lady stood at the edge of the ballroom, her expression thunderous, and gestured them out the door as they were stepping off the dance floor.

Mairi complied meekly, knowing that she and Connall deserved a thorough dressing down. From the countess's perspective, they'd behaved abominably with that wild dance. But that was not what happened when all five of them were finally in the carriage.

Instead of glaring at her and Connall, the countess turned her wrath on Sadie and Iseabail. "Have you two lost your minds?"

The girls each opened their mouths to say something, but neither got a word out. The countess lifted her hand to silence them and began listing the stories surrounding girls who wandered away from their chaperones. Every one came to an unfortunate end.

Clearly Sadie and Iseabail had done something risqué, but no exact details came out. Eventually, Connall spoke, his low voice easily interrupting the countess. "I will hear the details of this tomorrow first thing. You are both under my sponsorship, and I will know the truth."

That was a mistake, especially since the countess was already furious. They all knew that Connall was paying for their Season, but money wasn't enough to get one into a *haut ton* ball. It was the countess who was their entrée into society. Without her, they'd get no invites, and whatever they did reflected strongly on her.

And so she told them in no uncertain terms.

"Your sponsorship!" the countess cried as she turned her fury on Connall. "You're hardly an example of moral fitness with that dance." She shook head in despair. "After all of you leave, I shall be the one back here having to face my friends after this day. It is I who am sponsoring all of you, and I expect every one of you to remember that."

Nothing to say to that, except to assure her they understood and would be on their best behavior from now on. Even Connall had the wherewithal to apologize for any offence. The countess received their words with skepticism, and who could blame her? Neither Mairi nor Connall regretted the spectacle of their wild dance. Whatever Sadie and Iseabail had done had put them in high color. Both seemed very pleased with themselves despite their bowed heads and demure expressions. And so it was no wonder that the rest of the ride home was filled with tales of women and a few men who had not listened to their elders and came to regret it.

As soon as they entered the home, the countess declared a headache and took to her bed. The girls took one look at each other and dashed up to their room. That left Mairi and Connall staring at each other in absolute silence.

Connall broke the silence first. "Do you know what the girls did?"

"I have no idea."

He nodded grimly. "Then it'll wait until tomorrow." His expression softened. "Mairi—"

"Wait." She said the word quickly, her heart pounding in her throat. She looked upstairs to where the girls could be heard bumping around in their room. "Let everyone settle first."

"I won't wait long."

"I know."

They were talking in a code that she didn't truly understand. She'd said yes to something. He was impatient for it. And though she wasn't stupid, the evening and their dance were too new for her to have fully adjusted to what had happened.

"I'm confused," she confessed.

"I'll explain it."

"You'll tell me what to do," she countered. "And you're always wrong."

"No, Mairi. I'm always right, but I have to wait eons for you to realize that."

She snorted her derision, but part of her knew he spoke the truth. The two of them never saw things exactly the same way. He was a man who negotiated multiyear agreements with neighboring clans. He balanced disputes between his clansmen, and he brought wealth to his people far beyond what any other clan had achieved. She looked to the immediate actions, at who was drunk, who needed to be fed, and who should do the work while another rested.

None of their skills translated to a London ballroom or the search for a mate. And yet here they were. She'd felt so lost before tonight, as if she floundered in a place that made no sense. But when they were together, sensations overcame her, and she had no control over anything.

Going from floundering to overwhelmed was not a good progression. She should turn him away, close the door, and gather her strength to make sense of the Marriage Mart one more time.

"Don't lock your door," he said in an undertone. "I'll come when the house is quiet."

She looked at him, not knowing what to say. He looked at her, his expression inscrutable, but then his lips curved in a way she knew so well. It was half mischief, half delight, and he brushed her jaw with his knuckles.

"Don't run away, Mairi. You've just arrived."

"I'm not running anywhere," she snapped, though she knew she lied. Inside she was running in circles. Nothing made sense and he was her only touchstone. And yet, surrendering to him meant madness.

He winked at her as he held out his arm. It seemed he meant to escort her upstairs, and who was she to refuse such a courtly gesture? She set her hand on his arm; he covered it with his own. And together they climbed the stairs. They were halfway up when she realized what they were doing. It would be much the same climbing the stairs out of the great hall in his castle. Lord and lady heading to bed.

Her feet hesitated, and he looked down at her with a question in his eyes. Was she alright? Did she need something?

"I'm not a duchess," she said, though where the words came from she had no idea.

"I'm not a duke," he returned.

Yet. His father still lived, though the days were numbered.

"I am the last of the MacAdaidhs," she said. "And a girl. On my marriage, the clan ends."

He shrugged. "Your father might yet remarry. Either way, you've a noble heritage behind you." She saw the questions deepen in his eyes. Why was she telling him things he already knew?

"We have a bet on which *other* lady you intend to wed."

He shook his head. "You are running away, Mairi. Your feet may be planted right here, but in your mind, you are bringing up excuse after silliness, all because you are afraid."

"Some things should be feared."

"And some things are only trying their best to help you."

Word games. Tangled thoughts. She was running, she realized, and every time she turned around, there he was guiding her in the direction he willed. Tonight, he took her to her bedroom door. He bowed over her hand, pressing his lips to her glove while his eyes held hers. His gaze never wavered, even when he straightened and took a step back.

"Don't lock your door," he whispered.

She wouldn't, but she didn't say that aloud. Then he spun on his heel and disappeared into his own bedroom. Down the hall, Mairi could still hear Sadie and Iseabail whispering to one another. She heard a thump, then a cascade of giggles.

She could head to their bedroom. She could hear the truth of this night from them and fall asleep in one of their beds while listening to their secrets. That would foil whatever kisses and more that she'd promised to Connall.

She didn't. She went into her bedroom, allowed the maid to help her undress, then quickly dismissed the girl. She tried to sit on the bed and wait but was too restless. Her nightrail choked her, so she opened the top few buttons. She opened the window, wishing to see the moon on the highland moors. The London city was close and cluttered with dim pools of lamplight. There was a charm to it, but it did not soothe her.

She wrapped her hand around the bedpost and leaned against it. What little breeze came in did little to cool her body. Summer was done, autumn begun, but she felt like she was burning up just from the frenzy of her thoughts.

What was she about to do?

CHAPTER EIGHTEEN

C ONNALL SLIPPED THROUGH the quiet hallway. It had been excruciating to wait until the house settled. He ought to wait even longer. He could still hear whispers from Iseabail and Sadie's room, but the lure of finally touching Mairi had him rushing his fences. Again. He risked losing her forever if he didn't control himself.

But the drive to have her was too strong. So he slipped through her cracked door and silently shut it behind him. He saw her then, standing by her window and outlined by moonlight. Her white nightrail was ghostly in the darkness, cut by the dark slash of her arms where she wrapped them around herself. When he shut her door behind him, she tilted her head to the side as if she listened or looked for something. But she didn't speak.

"Are you afraid, Mairi?" he asked.

"Yes."

"Of what?"

She didn't answer. He knew that she did not like declaring one thing or another if she was not sure of herself. But in this, even a fool could see she had doubts. He crossed to stand behind her, then waited a moment. She needed time to accustom herself to his presence and his heat. Then he gently set his hands upon her shoulders.

He felt tension there, a tight stillness to her body. But she did not flinch away.

"This is pleasure, Mairi. Nothing more. I can give you a quickening. Happiness like you have never experienced before, and yet you will ride it. You will see that there is nothing frightening in one's body."

He kneaded her shoulders, willing them to soften.

"I know what a quickening is, Connall. I have experienced many."

He jolted, surprised enough that his hands stilled. "Who did such a thing with you?"

She twisted until she faced him. "I did, you idiot. Do you think a woman cannot know these things by herself? How old were you when you first stroked yourself for pleasure?"

He frowned. "Boys discover it young."

She shrugged. "Girls may learn of it later, but we do learn."

She was facing him now and he could see the defiance in her face. So fierce, even when so unsure. "Then you have never had a man…?"

"No."

He would be her first. That made his cock surge with pride. She noticed. Hard to miss given that he was wearing his kilt and naught else.

"Why are you in your tartan?" she asked.

"Because I should be when I claim my woman."

Her eyes widened and she shied backwards. "So this is it now? We couple tonight and are wed?"

"That is the Scottish way."

"Maybe. If we were in Scotland."

"You and I need no more than that. An agreement between us tonight. We can say our vows back home, and we can be done with all this prancing about London."

"What if I like prancing about London?"

"Do you? Because you have not so far. Have you met any man worthy of you? I don't believe so. And I have not seen any woman that can match you." He cupped her face. "Why do you fight what has always been between us?"

She closed her eyes, nuzzling into his hand. Her body swayed toward him, and he nearly caught her. But she pulled herself back before he could. She wanted him as much as he wanted her. And yet, she straightened away from him.

"I will not marry you this night."

"Mairi," he said, frustration making his voice gravelly. "Have I not been patient enough with you? Have I not given you time to see what is here in London? Have I not watched in fury while every soul in London picked you apart until you were a shadow of yourself?"

"And who are you to decide when time is enough? It's been three weeks and much of that was spent in preparation."

His hand tightened along the back of her neck. Not hard enough to hurt, but enough to make her guess the struggle he fought to control himself around her. She stood before him in her nightrail. He was in his kilt with a staff full ready to take her. But he held his body back for her sake. He did not hold back his words.

"It's been nearly ten years since I decided on you as my bride. Ten years of waiting for you to see that Liam was not meant for you. I let you find your way in his castle when it should have been in mine. I've been dancing to your tune for ten long years, Mairi MacAdaidh. When do you join me to dance in mine?"

She shook her head. "You want a wedding between us to-night? Because you made me laugh at a dance? Because I said yes to your smile and your broad shoulders? Because you are pretty, and I am alone."

"Ach! You are not alone! I am right here!"

She lifted her chin. "I will not wed you tonight."

"Mairi, what do you want? What will it take for you to see that this is the way it should be?"

She arched her brow at him. "Because you say so?"

"Aye! You are MacAdaidh. The last of a fine and noble clan, one that fought bravely at Culloden and none will say aught against them."

"And you are Aberbeag. Collaborators who would give none to the fight. Your grandfather received a dukedom for his betrayal of Scotland, and you—"

"I had naught to do with that. I wasn't even born yet, and I have done everything I can to reclaim wealth and honor for Scotland."

"For the Aberbeag, you mean. You seek to lessen the tarnish of your name by marrying mine."

He blew out a breath. "That is not why I want you." But it was why his father wanted her in the family. He had never told her that, but perhaps she already knew. Either way, he would not bring another soul into a discussion that should be between husband and wife.

She turned from him. "You are too much for me," she whispered. "Too much."

"And you are running away again." He set one hand on her shoulder, then let is slide down her arm. "This is naught but maidenly fear. You have experienced a quickening by yourself. It is a frightening thing to allow a man to do such a thing for you." He stepped closer until her heat burned the very air he breathed. "Or is it me you fear? Do you think that I will take what you will not give?"

"You are the man with a staff the size of a tureen."

A tureen? He didn't know whether to be insulted or complimented.

"I can feel it poking at me," she continued. "Where else has it been, Connall Aberbeag? What other women have you plowed? And why didn't you marry any of them?"

"If you wish, I can give you a full accounting tomorrow. I will tell you about women I can barely remember, the doxies who greet every young man with coin. What do you think men do when they visit Edinburgh?" He let his hand caress up and down her back. "I have not gone there for that in years."

"I will not marry you tonight," she said, her words decisive.

"Then let us do something partway," he said. "So you can feel what it is like with a man and not be afraid." He pressed a kiss to the back of her neck and was pleased when she tilted her head down to feel it better. And so he nibbled while she stilled. She didn't tremble until he brushed the scruff of his beard against her.

"It is not a marriage," she said.

"Not a marriage."

"You will not take my virginity."

"I will keep you pure, Mairi. I swear it." And when she didn't say anything, he pulled her back until she lay flush against him. "And you," he growled in her ear, "will not let another man do this with you. Not until all is settled between us."

She snorted. "As if I would risk this with anyone else."

He grinned. That was the closest she had ever come to admitting the connection between them, and the joy that suffused him was enough to make him bold. He was still careful to hold a steady pace, but the terms had been set now. He could touch her as he willed and bring her to a peak that she had never had before.

He swore it.

And so where before he had been stroking her back, he wrapped his arm around her belly. He spread his fingers wide so that she could accustom herself to the size of him in front and behind.

"When it is time, lass, we will fit. I promise you that."

"Not tonight," she said, her voice tight.

"Aye. Not tonight."

Then he let his hand stroke upward. He filled his palm with her breast. He enjoyed the weight and the size of it while measuring the cadence of her breath and the tightness of her nipple. He felt her roll her shoulders back and down, stretching to give him more room to play. Easy enough to lift his other hand and possess her other breast. The fabric was in the way, but he used it to chaff her nipple when he did not want to squeeze it yet.

"It is different, isn't it?" he whispered. "When a man's hands cover you."

He heard her swallow before she spoke. "You're verra big, Connall."

"You are a match for me."

He shifted his hold then, moving to unbutton her nightrail. The fabric came apart easily, one button releasing at a time until the garment draped across her upper arms and bared her breasts to his caress. Flesh upon flesh then. His hands were calloused, and her skin silky smooth. He stroked her, touching as he willed, waiting for the catch in her breath as she leaned back against him. She liked it best when he tugged at her nipples. She whimpered when he twisted them. And then he kissed along her neck before whispering into her ears.

"Here's something I'll bet you could not do."

"What?"

"You've not had a man's mouth there. You've not learned what a man's tongue can do."

She had no response to that. He knew her fears threatened to choke her sometimes. This would be indecision as well as fear, so he kept her too busy to argue. He twisted her and set her hand on the bedpost.

Her nightrail fell to her elbow on that side, but on the other, it dropped down to her waist and she shook her arm out of the sleeve. What a glorious sight to see her so before him. Her breasts bared to him and her posture strong. Her eyes were wide, and he thought he could see the beat of her heart tremble at her neck. But it was her breasts that drew him. And the desire to hear her whisper, *yes*, again.

He kissed the swell of her breasts, then lowered his mouth to her nipple. He teased it with his tongue, then sucked it inside his mouth. Sharp pulls made her gasp. A nip of his teeth had her free hand brushing into his hair. And when he added strokes with his hand on her other breast, she swayed where she stood.

He looked up and smiled at her, pleased to see a dazed look on her face. Her eyes were wide and her lips parted.

"It's lovely, isn't it?" he asked. "What a man can do that you cannae?" His brogue was returning as his own blood soared.

"Aye," she said as she looked at him. She still had a hand in his hair. She brushed through his locks and stroked down his jaw. "Is...the rest different, too?"

"That's what we're going to find out, yes?"

She took a shuddery breath. "Yes," she said, then she released the bedpost and let her gown drop to the floor. She stood naked before him, and he was overcome by the beauty of her. Full breasts, narrow waist, the flare of her hips to cradle a babe, and the muscular strength of her legs. He saw the future in that moment. Here was a woman to stand tall by a man, adding to his strength as they built a good life. From her body would spring healthy children who would grow into powerful adults. She would be the wellspring that nurtured them, and he would be the man who kept them safe.

The image flooded him, and it was all he could do not to drop to his knees before her in worship. She was everything he wanted in one beautiful package.

"Connall?" she whispered.

He couldn't speak, so he let his body do the talking. He leaned forward and swept her off her feet. She gasped in surprise but kept the sound muted.

He set her down on her bed and followed down immediately afterwards. He needed to kiss this woman. He needed to taste every inch of her. He needed to spread her thighs and plant himself so deeply in her they were joined together forever.

"Con—"

He cut her word off with a kiss. He thrust inside her mouth as if it were his tureen. He plunged in, he conquered her tongue, and he stole her breath from her. So fevered was his possession that he resented that they could not remain joined like this, sharing breath and life without an inch between them.

That could not be sustained. He had to break from her lips, he had to let her inhale apart from him, and so he pressed his mouth to her neck. He pressed his tongue against the pulse point in her neck. And he kissed his way back down to her breasts.

She was not passive as he lathed her nipples. Neither was she silent. She writhed beneath him and wound her hands in his hair. She whispered his name until she finally clenched his hair in her fist and yanked him back.

"Connall!" she hissed, her breath short and tight.

"Mairi?"

"Too much! Too…" Her breath was slowing. "You are too much."

"You cannot control this," he said. "This is a horse that gallops free."

"Connall—"

"I will not lose control. I swear it." He gently disentangled her fist from his hair. "Trust yourself with me."

"I trust you," she said, though her words sounded strained.

"Then there is nothing to fear," he said.

He smiled at her then swooped down to kiss the side of her breast. It was a playful gesture, and she smiled when he looked back at her.

"What if…" she began but could not finish her question.

"What if I betray you?'

"No. Not that."

"What if you like it?"

She bit her lip. "You know I do."

"Then there is nothing more to say." He kissed her breast again, this time closer to her nipple. He nipped her skin, teased her flesh, and waited until she smiled at him.

"I am afraid to let go."

"I know."

"I am afraid it will feel better than anything I have ever experienced before."

"It will."

"I am afraid no other man will make me feel as you do."

He grinned at her. "You can be sure of that."

She chuckled as she touched his face. He could tell she was

struggling with her thoughts, and he waited a moment more. He quickly realized she didn't want to think. She had needed the time to face her fears, and now she needed to let him do as he willed.

"Just feel, Mairi. That is all you need to do."

So saying, he bent his head to kiss her again. This time he worked her breasts slowly with teeth and tongue. Her heart pounded loud enough that he could hear it, but he did not stop. He began to move in time with her breath. He stroked her as her body began to move, arching her back, twisting her feet. He increased his attention to her then, squeezing her nipples until her breath caught on a sob.

That was too much for her, so he eased off. He gentled his caresses and stroked down her belly. Her heart slowed, her breath evened out, and soon he was nipping at her mound. For sure she never felt that, but he did not dare push her so hard tonight. Instead, he let his hands slip between her knees. He spread her apart and nearly swooned at the heated scent of her.

He could not resist touching the silk of her thighs, but he waited to give her a chance to change her mind. Instead, she smiled at him.

"Your hands are so large," she said. "I like them."

That was all the permission he needed. She wanted to feel his hands in her quim, and he was all too willing to comply. He pushed further up her thighs. And when he finally trailed his fingers through her moisture, she exhaled as if she had been waiting forever for this moment.

He studied her body as he touched her, learning every quiver and gasp. He saw her mouth circle into a surprised O while her eyes widened. He listened to her breath, and he saw her skin flush. She whimpered when he pushed his fingers inside her. Her eyes fluttered when he rolled his thumb across her peak.

He moved faster now, letting her scent consume him. Her desire fed him while his need to see her orgasm drove him. How he longed to do more than just stroke her, but he held himself back. Instead, he plunged his fingers into her. He felt her body tighten around him and he rubbed her peak with such pleasure.

She grabbed a pillow without him prompting her. She pulled it to her face to muffle the sound. And so he was left to feel her legs tighten, her body undulate, and her breasts shake. Until the moment she went completely wild.

Such strength as she gripped him. Such wildness in her while wracked with pleasure. He wanted to prolong it forever, but she scrambled back from him. The pillow fell off her face, and she stared at him wild-eyed as her body continued to pulse and quiver.

"Come here," she whispered.

How could he resist? He came forward, kissing her with all the desire pent up inside him. To see her come had been glorious, but now he burned for her a thousand times more than before.

She kissed him back, one arm wrapping around his neck. The other hand stroked his arm and his chest, and then down to his cock. She fumbled through his kilt to get to him. And though she was clearly inexperienced at this, she had a firm grip.

He pulled away from her but didn't argue. Her hands were on his body, and she was naked before him, still flushed from her own pleasure. So he taught her what he liked. He wrapped her hands around him until his entire body hummed to the movement of her grip.

She worked him as she did everything—with complete attention and a brusque kind of love. He enjoyed that in her. He had never wanted a delicate flower of a wife, but a lady hewn in Scotland who could give as good as she got.

And so she worked him and he surrendered to her ministrations. He watched her study his form and knew when she understood what set him on fire. All too soon, he was ramming himself into her fist. The peak hit him like a lion's roar made all the more powerful because he held it back. It bounced around inside him growing stronger with every second's delay. In the end, he set his face to her neck, pressing sound into her as it shot through him and out.

Heaven.

And when it was done, she grinned at him as if she'd won a great prize and was well pleased with herself. It couldn't be better than what he felt. He was suffused with pure happiness.

"Not so bad, is it?" he murmured against her skin.

"Not so bad," she agreed.

They lay there together for a time while he caught his breath. Then she helped him clean up the mess, and he eased the embarrassment of it by murmuring how beautiful she was to him. Compliments stored in his mind from years of envisioning this very moment.

"Ack, enough," she said, but he could tell she was well pleased.

But then time began to tick between them. An awkwardness appeared. Did he lay next to her now? Were they to be wed? He knew the answer to the latter. With her, it was always "not yet." But tonight, he realized that it wasn't him she feared, but herself. And that no man could fix. She had to grow comfortable with her own desires.

Best to leave her wanting. Best to go now and let her think on their time together as perfect. But he couldn't make himself leave. The house was silent, thank God, so no one was listening except the two of them. He stretched out on her bed, tucked her close to his side, and forced her to speak truth to him.

And she let him.

CHAPTER NINETEEN

THE MAN SHOULD be sneaking away. They'd done what he came for, or so she thought, and yet, he was tucked in beside her as if he meant to stay. And Mairi was honest enough to admit that she wanted him to stay, too. She'd heard tales of men who slept directly after their fun was done, and though Connall looked at her with eyes half-closed, it wasn't because he was sleepy. He was thinking, just as she was, and the two of them were likely ensnared by the same questions.

What would that have been like if they'd done as married couples do? If she'd said yes to marrying him tonight?

It would have been glorious. But what would she think when it was done? Would she feel trapped? Afraid? She didn't know. And yet, she was reassured when he stretched out beside her on the bed.

Still, she would not feed his pride, so she pushed at his chest. "Ack, you're too big."

"I am perfect, just as you are," he said. Then he wrapped his arm around her and pulled her tighter still. She smelled the scent of his skin, the musk of his passion, and heard the steady beat of his heart. He was a solid man in all the best ways. Strong body, a patient lover, and not one to act without thinking. She admired that in him and knew how rare that was.

"That's nice," he said, his voice a rumble beneath her ear. She had no idea what he referred to, but she didn't argue because it was nice.

She relaxed against him. Her mind was still caught up in the wonder of a quickening with Connall. It had been wonderful, but it was also not enough. Her womb had felt empty as it clutched greedily at his fingers. She had wanted his full cock inside her, and that thought frightened her as much as it interested her.

Obviously, she wanted Connall Aberbeag in her bed, and what a foolish creature she was to desire such a thing. If she gave in to him, what part of her would be left? He defeated her at every turn, so much so that she began to like it.

"Now tell me," he rumbled beneath her ear. "What bastard taught you to fear a man's touch?"

"Ach," she sighed, no restraint on her brogue. "Yer like a dog with a bone. Leave it be."

"I will not," he said. "You've a fine man in your bed, Mairi MacAdaidh, and he'd like to know why you're afraid."

"I'm not afraid of you," she said, her voice hard.

"I know," he said. "And that makes it worse." He stroked his hand down her back, the sheer size of it reassuring as he touched her. "You're not a timid woman, Mairi, and yet in this—"

"No," she said, hating that he was pulling her away from sweetness to a place she didn't want to discuss.

"Mairi—"

"There was no one," she said. It was the best answer she could give. "I am a woman. That is reason enough to be cautious."

She felt him struggle with her words and no wonder. Her fear was illogical and mayhaps she'd think of it more in the morning. But for now, she was stretched out beside him. She felt his naked flesh against hers because she'd not bothered to put the nightrail back on. She had no wish to discuss something that was foggy in her own mind.

"Very well then," he said, giving in with a grumbling discontent. "Let us speak of what you're doing in London."

She snorted. "I'm looking for a husband."

"You have one right here. No need to look anymore."

She chuckled. "Not an ounce of doubt in yer whole body, is there?"

"Not about this." He squeezed her as he spoke, and she returned the gesture without thought. And when his arms relaxed, he dropped his chin on the top of her head. "Tell me what men you have seen here that you like. Is it that Mr. Day? The one who begged for a third dance with you last night?"

She rolled her eyes. "I can circle the man's whole arm with one hand. He'd break the first time I asked him to pick up a pot."

"I don't think he plans to help in the kitchen."

She snorted. "Then he best find a woman with more money than I, because he hasn't any of his own." That wasn't exactly true. There were rumors about his wealth, but none were proven one way or the other. "What of you? You were making eyes at Miss West."

He groaned. "I was eyeing that dress. So many ruffles. It made her look—"

"I know how it made her look," she interrupted. It made the woman appear like she had six bosoms and they all were thinner than a dead cat's teat. "It's her mother that makes her dress that way. No eye at all for what would help her daughter."

He grunted. "Marrying that girl will be marrying the mother, and that is something no sane man would do."

She couldn't disagree.

"What do you think of Lord Heath?"

Aaron's cousin? "The one who manages the food and drink at Carlton House?"

"Aye. I've met with him twice now about Liam's whisky. He seems like a good man. You met him at the theater two nights ago."

She remembered a large man with a warm smile. There was a sadness in his eyes that struck her as odd, especially given his general pleasant demeanor. She found out from the countess that he had lost his wife recently to childbirth fever, and now he was a widower with two small children.

"He's too sad. I've never been able to cheer a man up. That's the only reason you want me. It's because I cannot make you unhappy no matter how much I scowl."

He chuckled. "That is the God's honest truth," he said, obviously not realizing he'd just said that was the only reason he wanted her. "But I wasn't thinking for you. Sadie would be a good match for him, I think."

"Sadie? Are you daft? She's raised her two brothers on her own and took care of that shrew of a mother. Now that she's free, you think she wants a man with two children?"

Connall grunted. "I think they suit one another. He's got love in his heart, and she needs it."

"He's got children in his home, and she doesn't need that."

He nodded slowly, clearly not convinced. It didn't matter. Sadie would pick who she wanted and not either of them.

They continued to talk for a long time. They discussed the people they had met, laughing when a tale became too ridiculous. Then he got her speaking about home and what she missed, which was very little.

"Not a thing," she declared. "Except for the smell of the heather and the first snowflakes on my cheeks."

"Naught else?"

She smiled remembering the way the children tried to steal treats from the kitchen as if the cook and all the maids were blind. She missed the sound of a stream swollen with snowmelt, and the hot taste of cider heated over a fire and spiced with whisky.

But mostly she missed having a place in Scotland. As the MacCleal chatelaine, she'd had a purpose and structure to her days. Here in London, she had yet to find her purpose. Indeed, she wouldn't find one until she had a husband to give her a role.

"You're not a restful soul, Mairi," Connall said. "You'll drive the Sassenach crazy with finding things for you to do."

"There's work in every home. It just depends—"

"On the man and the home."

He fell silent then, but she understood his thoughts nonetheless. There was work for her to do in his castle. A place for her in his bed, too. But he held himself back, and for that she was grateful. Especially since she'd thought enough for one night. Felt more than enough, too. It was time for sleep, and her yawn made that clear to both of them.

"I must go to my bed," he said. "Or I'll be found here in the morning."

"Aye, you must," she agreed. Damn it, she was reluctant to move. So much so that he remained longer than was appropriate. Indeed, she felt his breath lengthening beneath her cheek and she poked him in the ribs.

"Don't fall asleep! We'll be caught for sure."

"Huh? Oh." Then he stretched against her, letting her feel every glorious muscle in his body and his lengthening cock. "Are you sure?"

"Aye," she said, forcing herself to move away. "I am."

He pushed himself upright then rolled out of her bed. But lest she think he had given up completely, he paused when he was directly above her. She was on her back then and still naked. How easy it would be to wrap her arms around him and draw him down. She could spread her legs and cradle his hips with her own. And so wet was she, he could possess her with a single thrust.

But she couldn't do that yet. Not if it meant she'd be bound to him forever. She didn't even know why, but she would not say yes, yet. So she lay still beneath him while he supported himself on arms and knees without touching her.

"Mairi," he said, his voice a low growl of hunger.

"Nay, Connall. I told you so."

"I know."

Then he kissed her. He didn't press his body down upon her but bent his arms enough to press mouth to mouth with her. He took his time with the kiss, seducing her with lips and tongue until she was panting with need.

And then he sprang off the bed like a young cougar leaping

onto a rock.

"Dream of me," he whispered. Then he grabbed his kilt and walked naked straight out of her bedroom.

She waited until the door shut silently behind him to answer. "As if I have done aught but that every night since you were seventeen."

CHAPTER TWENTY

CONNALL WOKE FEELING energetic for all that he got very little sleep. That's what Mairi did to him. She energized him even when they were fighting. Especially when they were fighting. But last night had returned him to the place where they'd once been as friends, before adolescence had muddled his thinking. Back then, they could talk about things, share things big and small, and laugh until their sides hurt. Certainly, Liam had been part of their trio, but Connall had always enjoyed a special connection with Mairi and now it seemed they might be approaching that point again.

Maybe.

If only the damned woman would talk to him. Something kept her from marrying him, and he was determined to find out what.

But first he had to find out what Sadie and Iseabail were up to last night. Which meant it was time to wake them in a very Scottish way. He knew both women had adopted the English way of sleeping well past noon. It made sense given how late the countess kept them out. But this morning, they were about to have a rude awakening.

He dressed quickly and even made sure to shave. He planned to visit Aaron's cousin today at Carlton House. A third visit to deepen the acquaintance. He still thought the man would be an excellent match for Sadie, but Mairi had sown doubts in his mind.

It wouldn't hurt for him to do more investigating there before he pushed Sadie in that direction.

Then once he was dressed, he crossed the hall with a great deal of pleasure. He rapped loudly on Sadie and Iseabail's door, then strode right in. He thought to startle them. He thought to impress upon them that he was the one paying their bills and they would damn well confess all or he'd make their lives miserable. He meant to intimidate them.

He got exactly one of those things. He certainly startled them both awake. What he didn't expect was that both women would leap out of their beds and attack as if he were the devil come to claim them. Sadie was the fastest, but Iseabail was the most vicious. His cousin leapt from her bed and landed on him with a screech so loud that it left his ears ringing. She didn't hurt him per se. Her fists didn't carry much punch, but they were very well placed. A tap to his eye, another to his neck, while the bulk of her weight landed on his torso. The combination was enough to have him staggering against the doorframe like a lumbering ox.

That's when Iseabail made her mark. There was plenty of power in her fist as she clipped him across the jaw. And then she kicked straight at his bollocks. He wished he could say he saw it coming and avoided the punch to his groin. Truth was, he couldn't see anything with Sadie still aiming fists at his face. He avoided Iseabail's kick because he was ducking away from Sadie. But together, the women had him scrambling out of their bedroom like a teenage boy caught sneaking in where he ought not be.

In less than a minute, he was on his arse with an arm raised to protect his face. He could have defended himself better, but he had no intention of fighting the women. All he could do was protect his important parts and pray they realized he didn't mean to hurt them.

Fortunately, they figured that out fairly quickly. But he didn't lower his arm until he heard Mairi's dry voice cut through the hallway.

"And let that be a lesson to you, Connall Aberbeag. You've no call to be bursting into anyone's bedroom much less two Scotswomen who know how to fight."

"I only meant to..." he began, but he quickly cut off his own words. What could he say? He meant to shock them? Intimidate them? Clearly, Scotswomen didn't intimidate so easily.

"Exactly," Mairi drawled. Then she cut the girls a hard look. "Get dressed. He's got a right to hear what nonsense you've been up to. You've punished him enough for being an arse. Now it's time to face yer music as well."

Sadie and Iseabail nodded, their fearsome expressions fading into guilt. "We'll be down—"

Slam!

One room to the right, the countess's bedroom door burst open, and the lady stood there in a pink, heavily flounced dressing gown. "What manner of idiocy is this? Screeching when the sun's barely up? Is this a Scottish holiday no one told me about? A ritual to wake the dead?"

No one spoke and absolutely no one mentioned that the sun had been up for several hours.

"Well?" the woman demanded as she glared at them all. "And why is his grace on the floor? Have some self-respect, Your Grace. Get up. You're a duke."

"Not yet, he isn't," drawled Mairi.

"As if that makes the least bit of difference," the countess snapped. "You're in my house and I'll not be woken in such a manner again."

Connall rose to his feet and bowed deeply to the countess. "It was all my fault, my lady. I was trying to get their attention."

"You got the whole neighborhood's attention, I shouldn't wonder."

"I meant to demand an accounting."

The countess glared at him. "For what?"

"Whatever they did to infuriate you last night."

The woman turned her hard stare at Iseabail and Sadie, and

then finally to Mairi. "Very well," she said firmly. "You may discipline them. And while you're at it, tell yourself to act appropriately when you waltz. Do the steps assigned as a proper duke or take yourself back to Scotland where such madness is probably considered normal."

What could he do but bow deeply again? "Yes, my lady."

The countess gave them all one last hard look, and then turned on her heel and went back into her bedroom. Connall waited until all was quiet in the lady's room. It took several moments. And then he turned hard eyes to his cousin and her friend.

"Downstairs. Library. Five minutes. That will be your last chance to convince me."

Sadie frowned. "Convince you of what?"

"That you two should be allowed to continue your Season here and not be sent back home."

Iseabail's eyes widened in horror, but Sadie knew him too well to be fully intimidated. "Connall, you'll not be—"

He raised a single finger. Thankfully he still held enough authority to silence her mid-sentence. "Downstairs. We'll not disturb the countess again." Then he turned on his heel and left.

⇛⇚

THE COUNTESS'S LIBRARY had been the province of her late husband, but that had been several years ago. A large desk dominated the back corner of the room, its top gleaming with fresh wax. But that was the only beautiful part of the whole room. Every other thing looked slightly shabby and rarely used.

A week into his sojourn in this house, Connall had taken this place as his own. And though he never disturbed what was already in the room, he'd set it to use. The desk now had a pile of letters he'd received from Scotland yesterday afternoon. A moment after Connall entered the room, the butler brought tea in and placed it on a table near the fire. And best of all, Connall had found a love of the chair behind the late earl's desk. It was soft and fit him well.

He sat and tried to pull in every ounce of authority he could. He'd barely sat down when all three women filed in.

Sadie and Iseabail took the seats directly in front of him. They both looked nervous and a bit ashamed, though Sadie, as usual, had a defiant tilt to her body. Mairi came last and settled in a chair by the fire. Near enough to hear, but not officially part of the interrogation.

He had a moment of pure pleasure seeing her there. That would be the act of a wife to the laird. She would be there to listen and support but would not challenge his authority. It made him smile at her until she blushed rose. And given the morning sunlight falling on her face, he could see every delightful shift in color.

"Would you rather we skip this?" Sadie drawled. "We are happy to raise our hands and swear never to do something so foolish again, aren't we Iseabail?"

Iseabail's hand shot up. "Never again," she said firmly.

Connall forced himself to look away from Mairi to glare at Sadie. "Tell me what happened," he commanded.

"Well…" began Iseabail.

"It was nothing," interrupted Sadie.

"The countess has it well in hand," continued Iseabail. "She's brilliant about these things."

Sadie nodded. "She was very angry and chastised us thoroughly."

"We've learned our lesson."

The patter went on for a tediously long time. Long enough for Mairi to lose her patience. "Oh, for the love of heaven above," she snapped. So much for being the silent lady who did not interfere. "Out with it. Iseabail, you first."

And so, the whole tale spilled out starting with poor Miss Duncan who was attacked by a blighter, Sadie's risky measure, and Iseabail's surprised participation.

"I don't regret it," Iseabail said. "It ended perfectly."

"Has it?" Connall asked. "Did the man die? Do you know what the English might do to a Scottish woman who killed one of their own? A darling son—"

"Do you know what he did? Do you know what he has been doing?" Sadie demanded.

"Do you think an English court will care?"

That silenced them all. They all knew that the courts were not friendly to women, and Scotswomen were even more vulnerable. He let them stew in that fear. He would have to find out what had happened to the man. He completely relied upon the countess to mitigate any damage to the girls' reputations, but she could do nothing to stop any more violent revenge. Given what he'd already heard of this Mr. Carr and Mr. Barrett, he feared that nothing would restrain them from seeking revenge in a more tangible way.

It was up to him to stop that, and that would take time and information. But in the meantime, he couldn't have Sadie and Iseabail thinking what they'd done was safe or even sane.

"Why didn't you come to me?" he asked. "I could have handled this—"

"Among men?" Iseabail challenged. "That's exactly why bastards like him exist. Because men allow them to."

Connall's eyes narrowed. "You don't know me well, Iseabail, so I will forgive you that statement. But do not think that I am anything like your uncle or his men."

"Then you know their character," she said.

"Aye."

"And you have done nothing for the people under his care." The way she sneered that last word sent shivers down his spine. Just what had she endured?

"His people are his. No other laird can interfere. You know that." He was risking a war between her clan and his just by sponsoring her now. Didn't she see that?

"I know that sometimes one must take matters into one's own hands," Iseabail returned. The woman had surprising steel, but he could not let such folly stand. It was too dangerous. But before he could say that Mairi cut in.

"This was not one of those cases," she said, her tone firm.

That was exactly what he was about to say, but it came better from her.

"You should have come to me," Mairi continued. "And the countess. We would have helped you."

So much for thinking they would rely on him to protect them. That was, after all, his job as the son of their laird. "You should have come to me," he said firmly.

"There wasn't time," Sadie said. "And the fewer people who knew, the better."

Mairi snorted. "That's dung from a verra stupid sheep, Sadie, and you know it. I would have helped."

"I would have taken care of it," Connall said his voice strong. "And not a soul would be talking about hanging Scotswomen!"

Rather than be impressed, all three women shook their heads.

"You're the only one talking about that," said Mairi.

"Wrong," he said. "Because I can assure you that Mr. Carr and Mr. Barrett are. And if one of them died last night? His parents are right now speaking very loudly about it." He pushed to his feet. "There's the noisy way of doing things and the quiet way. You've chosen to go verra loud, and we won't know the end of it for a while."

He stopped a moment to stare hard at Sadie and Iseabail. Both were chastened, but still firm in their belief that they could withstand any repercussions from their actions. He hoped it was true. Indeed, his plans for the day now revolved around making sure of it. But first he had to say one last thing to Mairi.

"I'm off to see if the blighter died. I give you leave to do as you will with them."

"Me?" she said rearing back with surprise. "They're your kinsmen. I've got—"

"More sense than they. Tell me true. Would you have done such a thing without talking with me about it first? Or the countess?"

Mairi took a breath, but eventually shook her head. "The countess knows society. She'd know best what would come from beating up a rapist bastard."

"And me?"

"I'd trust you to watch my back. Two women in the dark against two men. They might be Sassenach dandies, but there's still danger there. It's only good sense to be sure a lucky punch won't have you as another victim."

Exactly. Their eyes met across the room, and he could see that she understood his thoughts. She had the sense of a laird's woman and a Sassenach duchess. He knew it even if she didn't.

"I'll not punish them, you know," she said. "If it were given to me, I would have done something to the bastard. Crush his bollocks at a minimum."

He nodded. He'd guessed as much, but she needed to understand that he trusted her judgement. "When I leave something to you, I won't interfere with your decisions." He sighed. "I've enough to do today to keep them from the gallows."

"And sell Liam's whisky," Mairi reminded him.

That, too. "When will you ever stop thinking of Liam?" he groused.

"When another man sleeps in my bed." She arched her brows. "He's the laird of my clan after his father. It's the proper way for me to think."

He looked at her a long moment, trying to figure out what she meant by that. After all, he had been in her bed last night. And while he stared at her, his expression caught halfway between confusion and hope, she flashed him a brilliant smile. It was her answer to his unspoken question.

It told him absolutely nothing. Except, perhaps, that she liked to keep him guessing.

He burst out laughing, a long full laugh that kept him filled with cheer. He smiled in the carriage. He chuckled when he went to speak with Lord Heath.

Indeed, he was in the best frame of mind until he learned that Mr. Barrett had indeed died. The son of an earl, dead as a doornail. And that was a verra bad thing indeed.

CHAPTER TWENTY-ONE

M AIRI WAITED UNTIL they heard Connall leave the library. The girls waited until he left the house. Mairi was still wondering what she should say or do with the barely repentant women when they heard Connall depart the house. And then, suddenly, the girls took the decision away from her.

"Well, that's done!" Sadie exclaimed. "Now for the important things."

Iseabail rushed forward. "Tell us everything. We saw your dance! At least part of it. Oh my!" She pretended to fan herself with her hand. "Thank goodness, the countess was in the cardroom or she would have fainted on the spot."

"Don't be daft," Sadie shot back. "She had to have heard while it was going on. She just pretended not to know. She's canny like that."

"Do you think so?"

"Definitely!"

Their conversation whipped between them so fast that Mairi was a little dizzy. She was also low on sleep, so that added to her difficulty. But then both women turned to look at her with excited eyes. "So? Tell us everything!"

"Everything? You saw us dance. After he was done swinging me all over and back, we had a proper waltz."

Sadie snorted. "Not that, silly."

Iseabail rolled her eyes. "We know that part. We're talking

about the *last night* part."

Mairi felt her gut clench as the blood heated her cheeks. She tried to remain calm. "I don't know what you mean," she lied.

This time Iseabail snorted. "We heard you!"

"We pretended to be asleep then listened at your door."

"You what?" Mairi gasped.

"Not for long. That would be rude," Iseabail said.

"Just long enough to know that he was in there with you. We heard you talk."

Oh no. No, no, no, no, no!

"We talked for a bit. About the Season and things. People we'd met. Nothing—"

"Liar!" Sadie said. She spoke with enthusiasm, not recrimination.

"Oh no," Iseabail said with a giggle. "I'm sure they spoke about that *too*." She gripped Mairi's hands. "Tell the truth now. Are you wed? Or about to be wed?"

"Stop, stop! I'm supposed to be here disciplining you, not being interrogated about something that did not happen."

Sadie giggled. "I bet it did. And you liked it!"

Mairi shook her head, but she couldn't resist the smile that curved her mouth. "We are not married. I am still pure. But we did..." She shrugged. "There was kissing. And mayhap a bit more."

"Ah," Iseabail said, feigning a swoon. "You're going to be a duchess."

"I'm going to be very cross with you both." Mairi needed to steer the conversation away from how she'd spent last night. "Why didn't you talk to me?"

Sadie waved her hand in the air. "And interrupt your wild dance? Don't be silly."

"You planned this far in advance of that dance."

"And you've been planning the social calendar with the countess, teaching us how to manage a household, and—"

"Kissing and things in your bedroom," Iseabail added with a

delighted whisper.

"And scowling at everyone when you're supposed to be having a good time," Sadie finished. She dropped her hands on her hips. "Really, Mairi, I would have gone to the countess before talking to you about this."

That stung. She would have helped them. She would have done whatever she could to put that blighter in his place. "You can always come to me," she said softly.

Both girls sighed as they each took one of her hands. "We know you're worried. We know you don't have a real dowry and that the countess has dropped all the work on you."

That wasn't true. Well, the dowry part was, but both girls were doing their fair share. "We have all been sharing the work—"

"But you fix it when we get it wrong. Which means you do your work plus ours." Iseabail squeezed her hand. "We're not angry with you. We're worried about you." She grinned. "At least I was until that dance yesterday. And the, um, *other things* you did last night."

"You really need to stop saying that."

"Not until you tell us about it."

Never. Not in a million years. Except, perhaps, to say, "It was...um..."

"Heavenly?"

With angels and harps? No.

"Romantic?"

Not really. It was emotional and difficult and wonderful all at once.

"It was good," she finally said. "Verra, verra good."

Both girls threw up their hands at that. "That tells us nothing!" Sadie accused.

"We want details," Iseabail pressed.

"You won't get them." Mairi withdrew her hands from theirs. "And let that be your punishment for doing something so reckless last night. What are we going to do if—"

"If what?" Sadie said in exasperation. "It was just a wee tap on the noggin," she said with a grin.

"And what if Connall's right and that's not the end of it? What then—"

"Connall's a worrier," Sadie snorted. "None of it ever comes to pass."

That wasn't true. Connall was the opposite of a worrier. "He takes the wildest risks and doesn't concern himself about the consequences."

"With himself," Sadie said as she dropped back down in the chair. "But he worries constantly about the clan."

"He sees every Aberbeag and worries about each one," Iseabail added. "Even I can see that. And that's a wonderful thing in a future laird."

Sadie nodded. "You didn't think it was his father handling the disputes, did you? Or negotiating with the other clans. It's been Connall for many years. His father gave him the running of things years ago."

"Gave him?" Mairi asked. "Or did Connall just take it?"

"Does it make a difference?" Iseabail asked at the same moment Sadie answered, "A little of both."

No, it didn't make a difference. But Mairi had to admit that she knew Connall mostly as the golden beauty who strode about on festival days. He was well-loved by everyone and reveled in the adoration. But Sadie had spent her whole life in his clan and knew the day-to-day Connall better than she did. "He's had the running of the clan?" she pressed. "For years?"

"Aye. And a good thing too because his father had a cruel streak. He could be petty and mean. But Connall stopped that and now the laird mostly sits around and talks with his pals."

Old men drinking and jabbering. Mairi knew about that. Then before she could say anything, Iseabail pressed her with an uncomfortable question.

"Are you afraid of the laird? That he's cruel?"

"What?" Sadie exclaimed before Mairi could answer. "The laird doesn't do anything now. He's too old and a bit daft. And

Connall's as fair as they come."

"He's generous," Iseabail contradicted. "He's sponsoring me, and he didn't need to."

"Right," said Sadie. Then she looked at Mairi. "So if it's not fear of the laird, and it's not because he's bad in bed, why aren't you marrying him?"

Trust Sadie to be the blunt one. The woman had no patience with subtext or subtlety. She wanted life to be black and white and fun all the time now that her mother was gone.

Usually, Mairi wholeheartedly agreed with such sentiment, but not today. Not about this. Today she was more like Iseabail in her silent watching of the world while plotting her next move. Except, in that, Mairi was also completely flummoxed. She had no idea what her next move was. She was just... she was... she felt...

"Mairi?" Iseabail asked. "You look like you're about to explode."

"I... I..." She dropped her head back to knock against the wall. "I don't want to love him."

The two women gaped at her. It was Iseabail who broke the silence first.

"Whyever not? I'd marry him in a heartbeat if he gave me a second look."

Mairi held up her hands in confusion. "I just don't. He's..." What? Perfect? Gentle? Irritating as hell? Sure of himself? Cocky? Damn, she had so many words for Connall, and none of them fit right. Or maybe all of them did. "I'm so tired of myself." And that was the truest statement she'd ever said. "Connall is wonderful, but I will not say yes to him." She shook her head. "It's madness. I don't understand myself."

Iseabail had no answer except to squeeze her hand in sympathy. Sadie, however, was of a much more practical mindset.

"I know why," she said firmly. "It's because you're so busy working all the time. You've got to do the meals for the countess, manage the money for your dresses, charm the Sassenach, and worry about us. You need to do nothing for anyone today."

"What?"

Iseabail clapped her hands. "A nothing day? What a marvelous idea!"

"What are you talking about?" Mairi demanded. "We're having a London Season. *Every* day is a nothing day."

"No," Sadie countered. "Every day is a husband-hunting day. That's different."

"Very different," Iseabail agreed. Then she cocked her head. "No wonder you don't want Connall right now. You'd be a laird's wife and a future duchess. There'd be no end of things to do all the time."

Sadie clapped her hands. "Then it's decided. Today is a nothing day. I say we start by wandering the shops."

Mairi shook her head. "I haven't any money—"

"We're just *wandering,* not buying. You'll see."

Iseabail grinned. "It'll be like a festival day."

Mairi snorted. "I worked three times as hard on festival days."

"Then today will be like a festival day you never had." Sadie grabbed her wrist and tugged her upright. "Come on. We'll have a full day of doing nothing. It's the best ever!"

There was no resisting them. They pulled her upstairs to dress for a day spent wandering Mayfair. They were in a carriage within an hour, then spent the day chattering like magpies who laughed about everything. A smart woman could see the edge of fear still lingering in Iseabail's eyes. A discerning woman could feel how desperately Sadie wanted to feel carefree. And an honest woman would say how much Mairi needed to not be smart or discerning right now. She had to be exactly what she was: a girl with nothing to think about and only fun to experience. At least for today.

"A nothing day," she said. "I like it."

They wandered the streets of Mayfair looking in shop windows, laughing at the antics of a dog with a showman, and smiling at gentlemen who tipped their hats at them. They never stopped to talk with anyone else though. Today was not for husband-hunting even at its most casual. Today was for them and it was the best day Mairi had had in years. One that had her laughing nonstop. One where she shared secrets about what had happened last night and how glorious it had felt. One where she admitted that Connall stirred her heart and her belly as no other man. And one where, amid the company of two girls, she finally allowed herself to think about why she had set herself so hard against Connall.

She didn't like the answer one bit, but she never got to discuss it. The confession was on the tip of her tongue when the unthinkable happened.

They returned to the countess's home to find the watch waiting for them. Or more specifically, for Sadie and Iseabail. It seemed Mr. Barrett had died. And in a most unexpected way.

CHAPTER TWENTY-TWO

"Stabbed?" Sadie gaped at the constable. "But we didn't stab him." She looked about the room feeling as if nothing here was real. She stood with Iseabail facing the constable and two watchmen. Mairi and the countess were here as well, but these rough men didn't seem to have any interest in listening to a bunch of women.

The squat, ugly constable frowned at them. "You are Scottish, are you not?"

"I am."

"Do you own Scottish knives?"

"Of course, I do. Bloody mad to not have one up in the moors."

"A knife was left by the body. It was a Scottish dirk. One that would be used by a lady."

"Doesn't mean it was mine!" Sadie exclaimed. "And we didn't stab him."

"And you certainly didn't bring any knife to the ball," stated the countess.

"We hit him with a tree branch," Iseabail said.

Sadie turned on her friend. If anyone was going to pay for whatever had happened, it would be her, not Iseabail. She'd dragged the girl unwittingly into her escapade. "*I* hit him with the tree branch. You punched him." She turned back to the constable. "And neither of us stabbed him!"

Mairi stepped forward. "Wasn't there another man there?"

"Mr. Preston Barrett," Sadie offered.

"Yes. Ask him. He'll—"

"Mr. Barrett is the witness against you. He said you stabbed Mr. Carr viciously with a horrible Scottish scream."

"A scream?" The countess cried. "At a ball? Don't you think other people would have heard?"

The constable folded his arms in irritation. "It was in the neighboring yard. Apparently, the orchestra was very loud."

"It was no such thing!" the countess snapped. "To think that you dare come to my house and accuse my young proteges of...of *murder?*" She shuddered as she said the word. "Look at them. They are young girls. They could no more murder a man than I could climb up the side of Big Ben."

The watchman to the left of the constable arched brows over his craggy face. "They look plenty strong to me. Bet they both carved up stags and the like for dinner, yeah? Little difference between cutting up an animal and a man. If'n a woman were pressed, and she didn't like it, she might stab a man. Several times, in fact."

"I might," Sadie said, her voice clipped. "But I didn't. Much easier to hit him in the head and walk away. Which is what I did."

Iseabail took hold of Sadie's arm. "What *we* did."

"Nevertheless," the constable said. "I've got my orders. You'll both be coming with me." He gestured to the watchmen who advanced menacingly.

Mairi stepped in front of them, but Sadie pushed her aside. She could defend herself. Except, apparently, she could not in this case. These three men had the law on their side. But when the watchmen each held up a pair of shackles, the horror of the moment hit her broadside. She was going to be set in irons?

"No," she whispered. Then more loudly. "Absolutely not! I did not kill Mr. Carr!"

The watchman opposite her grinned. "We can put 'em on you easy or I can put you on the floor, and I won't be gentle about it. We're in the light o' day now, Billy Bitch, an—"

"What did you just say?" A loud male voice cut through the room.

All three men straightened up at the inherent authority in the voice. The women did, too, though with less trepidation. For them, he was someone outraged on their behalf. Or at least so he appeared as he strode into the room.

"An' who are you," the constable sneered, "to interfere with the law?"

"I'm Lord Heath, and I've just come from Carlton House to save you from a huge mistake."

If they'd straightened at his tone, it was nothing compared to what the watchmen did at the mention of Carlton House. They snapped to attention so fast that their spines cracked, and no wonder. This man was an intimate of the Prince Regent, and only a fool would contradict him now. And yet, apparently, the constable was a fool.

"Don't care who you know. These women are wanted for murder."

"Yes, I'm aware."

Connall entered the room a moment later, and though his expression was relaxed, his eyes held a gleam of deadly intent. "I was meeting with him when we heard the news," he said by way of explanation. "Lord Heath insisted on coming here. Like the Prince Regent, he's very invested in all people in His Majesty's kingdom getting along. A false accusation of murder would be a disgrace that the prince would take very seriously."

Lord Heath nodded his bald head. "Very seriously indeed." He held up a knife. A long dirk with a silver twist knot handle. It looked very lovely with its exquisite metal work. At least as far as Sadie could tell. "Is this knife near the same length and weight of the murder weapon?"

The constable glared at the thing. "Yes. Deadly and light enough to be wielded by a woman."

"Hmmm. Really?" He passed it to Sadie. "Please attack me

with that, Miss Allen."

"What?"

"Come, come," he said straightening up to his full height, which was significantly taller than her. "I'm making improper advances. Defend yourself."

He wasn't making improper advances. He was standing there with his arms spread wide as if inviting her to gut him.

"I swear I will not hurt you," he said, his tone light and a little mocking, as if she couldn't possibly hurt him. She was no warrior, but she'd used a knife before. She knew where to strike a man and how.

But there he stood with a congenial expression on his broad face. He also had a broad chest and shoulders that would do any man proud. In short, he was a very large man with a bland Sassenach expression. What that meant wasn't exactly clear in her mind except that he seemed English through and through, and he was asking her to attack him.

She stood there stupefied. Did he really mean—

Apparently, he did because he suddenly lunged for her. He was faster than a man his size should be, and his hands were very large where they went for her body. Both hands on her shoulders, gripping her tight as he drew her improperly close.

She reacted on instinct, bringing the knife up between them. All she needed to do was point the thing toward his gut and shove. Except the moment she began to do that, he twisted his arm around hers and knocked the weapon wide. Indeed, the action was so quick she lost hold of the weapon. The thing went flying straight at a watchman who knocked it away with a quick flick of his wrist.

Damnation. She was a better fighter than that. And much too smart to allow him to twist her fully around until she was pressed back to front against him. Heavens, the man's heat was startling as he surrounded her.

What had just happened?

"You caught her by surprise," the constable said. "Any woman can take a man unawares."

"Really?" Lord Heath said. He turned around such that his back was to her. "Come at me again."

"What?" she said.

Connall grabbed the knife off the floor and offered it to her. "Attack him again, Sadie. And do it like you mean it."

"I meant it last time," she grumbled. But she'd been slow then. This time she was prepared, so she lifted the dirk in her fist. Damn, the point was really sharp. She did not want to hurt Lord Heath, but her blood was up. She would not stab down, but she would catch him.

She lurched forward only to have him duck away as he twisted to the side. Then in one smooth motion, he straightened up to catch her on the wrist. His hand was massive, and he easily held her away from him. Then he slowly, inexorably, tightened his fingers into her wrist. She tried to keep hold of the dirk. She really did. But there was no fighting the pressure as he squeezed.

The dirk slipped from her grip and fell into his other hand.

"So you've some skill in a fight," the constable said. "Doesn't mean Mr. Carr does."

"On the contrary, he spars at the same place I do with Gentleman Jackson. He is well-trained. Much better, I imagine, than Miss Allen."

"He *was* well trained, my lord," said the constable. "Now he's dead. Stabbed thirteen times, by the look of it. By someone who hated him."

"And you think it was her?" Lord Heath asked, shock in his tone. "By all accounts she'd just met the man. She's barely been in the city for more than a few weeks. Why would she be moved to kill a man with such venom?"

The watchman nearest Sadie spoke up. "She's a mad Scot. Savages, every one. Who knows what they teach their women?"

Mairi huffed out a disgusted breath. "We're not taught to kill men for grabbing a tickle. We're taught to kick 'em in the bollocks."

"Or hit him with a branch," added Iseabail.

Lord Heath waved away their comments as if they were of no

account. And maybe in his world, women had nothing of value to add. Sadie truly wanted to be insulted by that, but he was here defending her, so she held her tongue.

"The point is, she hasn't a motive for killing the man."

"He made lewd advances!"

Truth.

Lord Heath rolled his eyes. "As does every randy boy with a title. You know that as well as I. If she killed every man who tried to tup her, you'd have every lord in London demanding her capture."

"I do have one," said the constable. "Mr. Barrett was very clear."

"Ah yes, about Mr. Barrett." Lord Heath held up the dirk. "This is the Prince Regent's. Do you know Mr. Barrett brought a nicely wrought dirk to Carlton House just three nights ago? To compare his with Prinny's."

Connall's brows rose as if surprised. "You're saying Mr. Barrett had a knife just like the murder weapon?"

"I am. And there's more. Do you wonder if perhaps Mr. Barrett had a reason to kill his dear friend and neighbor?"

Connall frowned. "If they were dear friends, then what motive could he have for such a vicious attack?"

Lord Heath grinned. "Well, that requires a knowledge of Mr. Carr's estate. You see, upon his death his title passes to his cousin, but that's just the title. His father is a baron, you know, and very proud of the fact. The land, however, is owed to Mr. Barrett's father. It was placed as security for a loan."

Sadie's mouth gaped open. "So on Mr. Carr's death, Mr. Barrett gets all his land?"

"Yes. There's been bad blood between the two families for generations. Neighbors aren't always good friends and the Barrett family is a tricky bunch. Pretends to be your friend, loans you money with generous terms."

Sadie folded her arms. "How generous?"

"Payable upon the son's death, the son being the heir and all.

Normal interest and the like, so it sounds like a neighborly thing to do."

Connall grunted. "Unless you're planning on killing the son."

Lord Heath shrugged. "Well, Mr. Carr was shagging every girl he could get his hands on. It's reasonable to bet that he'd get a disease sooner or later."

Iseabail pressed her hand to her mouth in horror. "But they appeared to be friends," she said. "He spoke kindly about Mr. Carr."

"Yes," Lord Heath said gravely. "There's a dark twist in that one. Spend enough time with the man and you'd see it too. He revered Mr. Carr as much as he hated him. There's a history between those two that started back in Eton. Talk to his schoolmates and you'll hear about several times when Mr. Carr became violent."

The constable appeared to be thinking. Finally. "A child's spat is not the same as a man committing murder."

Lord Heath nodded. "But that makes much more sense than a slip of a girl stabbing a stranger thirteen times just because he'd tried for a kiss." He looked at Sadie. "Did you say you were going to tell anyone about the attack? Perhaps involve Mr. Barrett in it such that his status in society was threatened?"

Sadie nodded. "I'd already aligned the women against them both. The countess helped. No one was going to invite them to any parties ever again."

Lord Heath nodded. "That would definitely infuriate Mr. Barrett. Going to parties was the only thing he had in his life, and that was because he was attached, socially speaking, to Mr. Carr. If Mr. Carr did something stupid—say, accost the wrong woman—and that threatened Mr. Barrett's standing with the *ton*?" The man shrugged. "Well, that would make Mr. Barrett angry. Indeed, I believe he'd be furious enough to kill."

Sadie shuddered. To think she'd believed Mr. Carr to be the dangerous one. And she'd left Iseabail with him! What a fool she'd been! Meanwhile, Sadie wasn't the only one having a revelation. It was clear the constable was beginning to see the logic as well. He clearly didn't want to, but everyone could tell he was coming around.

"Well," inserted the countess with an airy wave. "It appears you have a bit more investigating to do before you come willy-nilly into a person's home to arrest innocent girls. I can't imagine what the broadsides would say if they knew you took the word of a murderer over myself, a future duke, and Lord Heath, who is very close to Prinny himself."

Of course, she could imagine it. They all could because the constable's career would be over the moment the first caricature began to circulate.

Still, the man had to get in the final word. He pointed a finger straight at Sadie's nose. "You're not in the clear, miss. Not yet. I suggest you not leave London until this is sorted out."

Sadie opened her mouth to answer, but it was the countess who responded first. "Not leave London? Of course, she's not going anywhere. We're in the middle of the Season. Do you want to see the stack of invitations we've gotten just today? We're headed to Almack's tomorrow, where Lady Castlereagh has asked specifically for us to attend. Most specifically. I swear I would never think of disappointing a woman so important to society or her husband. Do you know Lord Castlereagh, constable?"

Flustered the man shook his head. "No, my lady. I haven't had the pleasure."

"I have," said Lord Heath. "He's one who thinks we must be careful not to add bad blood with the Scots. He's right, of course. There's been plenty to do fighting the French. No need to cause disruption with the Scots without good cause."

"And proof," added Connall darkly. "Real proof." He snapped his fingers as if he'd just remembered something, then opened the door to the parlor. "I almost forgot." A maid came in carrying two dresses. "Constable, do you think stabbing a man thirteen times would be a messy business? Ladies, are these the gowns you wore last night?"

Both Sadie and Iseabail said, "Yes."

He turned to the maid. "Have these been washed yet?"

"No, my lord," the maid said with a curtsey. "I haven't had time what with preparing their dresses for tonight."

Connall passed them to the constable. "As you can see, there's no blood on them anywhere."

The constable made a show of inspecting every corner of their gowns, but everyone could see he was defeated. In the end, he passed the dresses back.

"I'll be looking into this deeply now. It's an important matter when a future baron is stabbed."

"A very grave matter," Lord Heath said. "Which is why it's important to catch the right *man*." He put enough emphasis on that last word to make the constable's face tighten. But even the two watchmen could see that they had the wrong suspects.

It took a little longer before they left the house. Lots of sour looks and a clear refusal to apologize. The countess was a lot more gracious than Sadie was. The lady showed the men out and talked blithely about misunderstandings and how appreciative she was that they tried to do a good job. Honestly, it made Sadie grind her teeth, but she knew better than to interfere. Plus, she had something else she wanted to say.

She turned to Lord Heath. "Thank you, my lord. It was very kind of you to help me like that. I am very grateful."

The man looked her up and down. If he appreciated her looks, he didn't show it. Instead, he shook his head in disgust.

"Don't be grateful," he said. "Stop being a bloody idiot. Even my six-year-old daughter knows not to wander off with strange men. And at a ball no less, and into the neighbor's yard. Do you know what could have happened to you?"

"I knew what I was doing," she said, somewhat peevishly. It had gone off perfectly. Or nearly so. How was she to know that Mr. Barrett was going to murder his unconscious friend? That wasn't her fault! And yet, Lord Heath laid this whole disaster at her door.

"You had no idea what you were doing," the man said, his

tone sharp. "You think that a man who casually rapes women wouldn't have other nasty tricks up his sleeve? Or friends who are angry enough to stab a person thirteen times?" He shook his head. "When you're at a ball, you stay at the ball." He looked at Connall. "I helped today, but you cannot count on that the next time she does something foolish. Hitting a man with a branch! Did you think to send someone to see that he survived? Head wounds are tricky. You might as easily have killed him. Indeed, you were lucky that Mr. Barrett decided to stab him first."

Sadie wanted to argue. She wanted to snap back at him that she'd planned her escapade carefully, except he had the right of it. She never sent anyone to check on the blighter. She'd assumed his murderous friend would take care of him. Instead, she settled for an angry retort.

"You've no right to speak to me—"

He didn't let her finish. He stepped right up next to her, towering over her until she felt like an errant child before him. He didn't touch her. He didn't need to. And while she was overwhelmed with the heated size of him, he spoke in a low tone.

"I am the man who saved you from the gallows, Miss Allen. I'd turn you over my knee if I thought it would get through to you."

There was no threat in his voice, but she heard the finality in his tone. Had she really been heading for the gallows? The idea terrified her. She'd lived an honest life. She was a respected woman back home. And yet here, she'd come very close to being hanged? The very idea froze her from head to toe.

And still he stood like a wall of disapproval in front of her. She might have accepted it from Connall. He was her clan leader and the one sponsoring her in London. And yet, this man dared to suggest he would spank her? That was a step too far.

Forcing strength into her body, she raised her gaze from his neatly tied cravat. She tilted her head back until she faced him squarely, if not exactly on the same level. And she spoke with an icy formality she'd learned from the countess.

"Your aid will be duly compensated, my lord. I'm sure my

lady's butler will have something for you on the way out."

His brows arched at that, and she thought she'd scored a true hit. Until his lips quirked in a sardonic smile.

"Miss Allen, you have no idea what my compensation entails." There was a suggestive note to his words, innuendo that made her cheeks heat even as her eyes dropped in embarrassment. Truly, she was grateful for his help. She'd erred badly last night and mayhaps he was the only thing that stood between her and a very awful time in prison, not to mention the gallows. But her pride kept her from owning her mistake to this man. Perhaps if he stepped back and gave her room to breathe. Or maybe if he weren't so large or smelled so damned interesting. She loved the scent of Bay Rum.

"Lord Heath," she began, forcing herself to be gracious. "I do appreciate..." Her voice trailed away as he spun on his heel. He bowed to the countess and then shot a look at Connall.

"We'll talk about that other thing tomorrow." He glanced back at her. "She's reckless, and that's idiocy for a woman on the Marriage Mart."

"Aye," Connall said. He said no more because Lord Heath didn't appear to need it. The man was already striding out the parlor door, leaving Sadie to stare after him while emotions roiled around inside her.

He'd been rude and impossible. He'd threatened to spank her. And he'd also gone well out of his way to save her life. He'd been brusque about it. Downright harsh, truth be told, but didn't she deserve that? If some stupid girl had come to Scotland and risked her life on a brazen stunt, wouldn't she give the girl a well-deserved dressing down?

But oh, how it stung.

She would take it today because she'd been caught off-guard. But woe be to Lord Heath if she ever saw him again. If he dared speak one harsh word to her, she'd tell him what she thought. By God, his ears would be ringing from the words she had for him.

But only after she apologized to everyone here for her reckless behavior.

CHAPTER TWENTY-THREE

THREE DAYS WENT by in a flurry of gossip and speculation. Thanks to the countess's guidance, all three girls managed to come away with their reputations intact. It did, however, cost them time. No gentleman was willing to show interest in any of them until after the hubbub cooled down. Which meant they went to parties, danced with the few men who offered, and smiled and smiled until Mairi thought her face would crack.

Which is exactly what happened on the fourth morning. Mairi had just approved Sadie's meal suggestions for the week when the countess slipped into the housekeeper's room where she'd been working. That the lady was awake this early was a surprise. That she was fully dressed and with a tight expression told Mairi that the discussion to come was going to be difficult.

As usual, she began with a smile. "Countess! What a pleasure to see you this morning."

"I'm not one to rouse myself unless it's important, so let the hour be a message to you about the urgency."

Mairi folded her hands in her lap and gave the lady her complete attention. "What do you wish to discuss?"

"It's time to make a decision," the lady said as she dropped down onto the empty chair set next to the fire. "Your time is up. Your money as well. You've got an offer, and so it's time to decide."

The statements were made with a kind of world weariness

that was the exact opposite of the face the countess usually presented to the world. Normally, the lady was all excitement and pleasure when in society, but today her expression was grave. And frankly, that was all Mairi could focus on. She hadn't the stomach to deal with the lady's other statements. But of course, she had no choice.

"Well?" the countess pressed. "What do you think?"

Might as well start with the easiest. "As to the money, I still have a copper necklace."

"Not after today. Madame warned me that the bill would arrive today, and she expects payment immediately. I cannot risk the other girls' chances upon you. If you were to refuse to pay—"

"Sadie and Iseabail won't get their gowns. I know. I understand."

"But you have an offer. That's good news. What do you think of him?"

Mairi tightened her fingers together. "An offer from whom? I haven't heard a thing."

The countess's brows rose. "Oh. I thought he'd spoken to you. I gave him permission to address you several nights ago." She took a breath. "It's Mr. Weissman, the barrister. He's the second son of a second son, but he travels in the best circles. Has a bright future ahead of him. You'd likely be tasked with managing his mother's home, but again, she's good *ton*. You'd be on the periphery for the most part, but you don't seem to enjoy the parties. And you'll have work to occupy yourself until the babies come. An organized wife is an asset to a barrister with aspirations, and you more than fit the bill."

Damned by faint praise. She was to be an organized wife.

The countess touched her hand. "Are you sure he hasn't spoken to you?"

"I am sure no one has asked me to marry him."

"Probably because of this business with Mr. Carr's murder." The lady shuddered. "But that should clear up the minute they find Mr. Barrett."

Apparently, Mr. Barrett had run the minute he'd heard the constable was looking for him. The man could be halfway to Russia by now. "I hope he is caught very soon," Mairi said, expecting just the opposite.

"I pray for it every night upon my knees." Then she pursed her lips. "Well, I'll try to prod Mr. Weissman today. Will you accept him?"

Good question. "Is he the one with the very large nose?"

"What? No, no. That's Mr. Tanners. And it's not that his nose is so large. Only that—"

"His face is somewhat small. Yes, I remember him telling me that. Though why he thought that was important is a mystery to me."

"He's telling you that his cock is normal-sized," the lady said with a wave of her hand. "Something about noses and male organs."

"Oh!" Sometimes the woman's bluntness was a welcome surprise. Sometimes it was just a surprise. "I suppose that explains his emphasis on the matter."

"I never put much stock in that myself. I'm told that a small cock can father a child as easily as a large one. But it's important that you know all the facts before making your choice."

This conversation was becoming very strange. "Thank you. But he's not offering for me, is he?"

"No, no. Though he wouldn't be a bad choice if you preferred him."

"I do not."

"Then we're back to Mr. Weissman. He's the brownish blonde one. Normal face, normal hands. Kind of stoop-shouldered, no doubt because of his work. Wears spectacles, too."

"The one with the bright yellow waistcoat? The dandy—"

"No. Mr. Weissman cannot afford to be seen as a dandy. That would be too damaging in a barrister."

Then who was it? "The one with the flat face and a nasally

quality to his voice?"

"Not him. The one you danced with last night. Or was it two nights ago? Oh bother. Never mind. I'll point him out to you tonight. I'm sure I can prompt him, but you'll need to answer right away."

Right away? "But why? There's at least a couple more weeks—"

"Because people are talking about you now. Better yet, you were never implicated in all that murder nonsense, so your reputation is in the clear except by slight association." Mairi opened her mouth to ask a question, but the lady waved it away. "Don't try to make sense of it. It's a delicate balance. Right now, you're part of the conversation. That's the best time to get a man to propose for fear that someone else will snatch you up. The last thing you want is for no one to remember you at all."

That made sense.

"So will you accept him?"

"I don't even remember him."

"You know the important things. He doesn't have any vices that I've heard of, you'll have something to do with your days, and there will be adequate funds to keep you on the periphery of society. What more could you want?"

Passion. Laughter. Love. Those were the words that filtered through her thoughts, but they were directly contrary to her stated purpose. She'd come to London with the explicit goal to get a husband who would keep her in a comfortable lifestyle without any of the difficulties of a boisterous, passionate Scotsman. This Mr. Weissman sounded like he fit the bill perfectly.

In fact, he was so boring, she couldn't remember him.

But what had sounded like the perfect husband weeks ago when she'd left Scotland in a huff, now felt like dining on milquetoast for the rest of her life. Meanwhile, the countess's expression softened into pity.

"Mairi, can you tell me what you're thinking? You were so

sure of yourself when you arrived, but now you seem listless and confused. If I didn't know better, I'd think you were languishing after someone." She didn't say more, but they both knew Connall was at the heart of her confusion.

"Did you love your husband?" Mairi asked, the question startling them both.

"I did. I do."

"And now he's gone and you're...?" She let her voice trail away into a question. By all accounts, the countess was blissfully happy in her place as a wealthy widow of good *ton*. And yet there were moments such as now when the woman seemed heart-breakingly sad.

"I am alone," the countess said, her voice low. "And that is worse than anything I can imagine." She forced a smile. "Which is why I fill my days with girls such as you. I want to usher you into the same kind of marriage I had."

"Mr. Weissman would not be a love match."

"Love!" the woman exclaimed. "Oh, I don't recommend those at all. Certainly, I was lucky in that regard, but what a woman needs is security. And that is exactly what Mr. Weissman will provide for you." She squeezed Mairi's hand. "I know it's hard to give up on girlish dreams of love and romance, but once you do, everything is so much easier."

Girlish dreams? Had Mairi ever had those? She didn't think so. Her plans had always revolved around running the MacCleal castle and making sure her father was able to keep shaping glass as it was the only thing left to him after her mother died.

Fortunately, the countess didn't seem to need an answer right away. She patted Mairi's hand as she stood up to go. "I'll point Mr. Weissman out to you tonight. We'll get him to propose right away, and then we can start planning the engagement party. It will be important for his family to see that you have the approval of myself and my family. It's never wrong to have a countess on your side, not to mention the titles my children have caught. They've all done very well for themselves, you know. Thanks to my guidance."

She waved airily as she left. Which left Mairi to stare after her and wonder what she was going to do. Normally she was so decisive, but whenever Connall came into her thoughts, everything became jumbled. Which meant she tried very hard to not think about him at all. Unfortunately, that no longer worked.

Especially when he joined them that evening. They were going to Vauxhall Gardens for an evening of dancing and delight. The countess specifically suggested it because it was a location that Mr. Weissman was sure to be able to join. He was not usually invited to events of *haut ton,* but tonight would be a perfect opportunity for him. And if Mairi wanted to accept his offer, they could wander down the Dark Path to discover if his "nose" was of an acceptable size.

That was exactly what the countess said as they gathered before departure. Mairi was horrified by the off-color joke. Especially since she made it right in front of Connall, who looked exquisite in his tartan. All that traditional Sassenach clothing had masked the breadth of his shoulders and the thickness of his muscles. He was a man who used his body, who could fight as a warrior of old or appear regal in evening attire suitable for the royal court. But in his tartan? No one could match his masculine beauty, and Mairi stood mesmerized by the sight of him.

"Mairi?" Sadie's voice cut into her thoughts. "Do you like Mr. Weissman?"

Weissman, who?

"His assets seem to match my requirements," she said, her mind somewhere else entirely. She was thinking that Connall's nose wasn't particularly large, but his cock certainly fit her needs. She couldn't forget the way his body had moved over hers four nights ago. That his kiss had brought her to shuddering release. Or that she ached to do that and more with him again. Maybe even tonight.

But how could she think that when the countess was intent upon her accepting Mr. Weissman's proposal tonight?

"I've let everyone know where we'll be tonight," the countess said as she shooed them out the door for the carriage. "We'll get you engaged tonight, I'm sure of it!"

Mairi could only smile and nod. No part of her had room to think of Mr. Whomever it was. All her thoughts were on Connall who sat across from her and watched her with steady, dark eyes.

"Perhaps we should take a walk," he finally said, "between the second and third sets. I heard the news of your father, by the way. I am very pleased for him."

Mairi jolted. If Mr. Weissman couldn't pull her attention off Connall, news from home certainly could. "News? What news? Is my father all right?"

Connall frowned. "He's very well, Mairi. I thought you knew. He has found a new wife. I am sure he has written to you."

"I haven't received anything." And why would Connall think that she could get such news and *not* tell him? Good lord, the man was as oblivious as a dolt!

"Finn must have arrived ahead of your father's letter."

"My father hates writing." She frowned, her mind spinning. "Finn's here?"

"He arrived this afternoon."

Oh yes. She'd thought she'd heard Finn's voice this afternoon but hadn't wanted to pry. The man was an Aberbeag. An important member of the clan, she believed, but she wasn't exactly sure of his duties. He had a distinctive roughness to his voice from an injury in a fight when he was a boy.

And none of that was important right now!

"What do you know of this woman?"

Connall made a futile gesture. "Nothing but her name. I thought to ask you about her!"

She glared at the man. "And *what is her name?*"

"Miss Juliet Adams. She's the teacher Liam and Clara brought in. It seems they have come to an understanding."

Apparently so, if they were about to marry. Or had married.

Good lord, such feelings were roaring through her, none of

them making sense. It had been a foundational part of her life that her father grieved the great love he had for her mother. That he cried over her loss every year on her birthday. That he touched Mairi's face with reverence and said how much she looked like her mother. And now he was replacing her with an English school teacher?

"Why didn't you tell me?" she whispered.

Connall huffed out a breath. "I thought you knew. And I meant to talk to you about this later tonight."

She shook her head, still trying to sort through her thoughts. "Why would he do this without talking to me?" It was a stupid question. She knew it the moment she voiced it, and so Connall made haste to point out.

"And why would he speak to you, Mairi? Especially when you left in the middle of the night to find a husband in London without a word to him?"

Truth spoken baldly. Mairi winced because he had a fair point.

"I was so angry," she whispered. "I didn't think."

Connall abruptly leaned forward. There were five of them in the narrow confines of the carriage, but the others were staying scrupulously quiet. It was Connall who reached forward and gripped her hands.

"He is not unhappy with you. Indeed, none of us were surprised by your temper. But if you are free to find your own future, then you must leave him to do the same."

She knew it was true, and yet the suddenness of the news left her feeling bereft. "Aye," she finally said. "You have the right of it." It was time to step into the next part of her life. Her father had found someone new, and so should she. "Countess," she abruptly said. "I believe I will accept Mr. Weissman's proposal tonight."

CHAPTER TWENTY-FOUR

CONNALL GLARED ACROSS the dance floor and cursed himself for a fool. Of all the stupid mistakes he'd made in courting Mairi, today's had to take the bloody cake. He knew that Mairi and her father had a special bond. It had been just the two of them since her mother had died in childbed along with her little brother. Through the years, Mairi and her father had struggled together, finding their place with the MacCleal clan and building the glass factory for which her father was so famous.

He should not have told her so baldly that her father had at last filled the emptiness in his life with a new love. Even though Mairi would want to see her father happy, such news could not be anything more than a blow. She was no longer the only woman in her father's life, and now she likely felt cut adrift.

That had been his purpose, after all, and his motives had been dark. He'd waited these last nights for her to come to him. He wanted her to choose him. Instead, all the talk in the carriage had been about getting Mr. Weissman to propose.

And who the bloody hell was Mr. Weissman?

Mairi's intended husband, apparently. And Connall was nothing but a discounted Scot who had laid his heart bare to her four nights before.

So he'd lashed out at her in his discontent. And now she was dancing with every damned man here as if her very life depended upon it. Her smile was rigid, and her laughter forced. She danced stiffly, and he could see that she was fighting her upset. Why didn't she turn to him when her father found a new woman to love? Why wouldn't she let him show her that she had another in her life who would adore her above all others?

Instead, he had wounded her, and now she danced with the Sassenach as if one of them were the key to her happiness. Worse, she'd declared her intention to wed the unknown Mr. Weissman, and Mairi never went back on her word.

What a fool he was.

But if he was a fool, then he might as well be a complete one. He had tried patience with the woman, attempted logic, and even seduction. None of it had worked, and so now he was going to do what he was best at: action.

He had said they would talk between the second and third sets. He'd thought that would give her enough time to see the lack of opportunities around her and turn to him. He was done with that nonsense. She was the only woman for him, and he would not leave her to another man. Not without staking his claim in the most Scottish way he knew how.

He would declare it boldly, leaving no room for doubt in anyone's mind. And let the damned Mr. Weissman decide how to compete with that.

He didn't even wait for the set to end. He knew the patterns of the dance and chose his moment well. Mairi and her partner were at the top of the formation. They spun around once, separated, then headed on opposite sides of the line all the way down to the bottom. Easy enough for him to wait near the top of the line, then grab her just as she spun away from the gentleman and straight into his arms.

"What—?" she gasped as he swept her around in another spin before setting her on her feet.

"You're miserable," he said to her startled face. "And you're always rash when you hurt. I've come to keep you from doing something stupid."

Her eyes widened and she abruptly set her hands on her hips.

"And who are you to decide such a thing for me?"

"I'm the man who loves you, you damned fool. And woe be to any other soul who dares challenge me for your hand." He swept a glare across the room and was pleased to see several gentlemen shrink away from him. He hoped Mr. Weissman was among them. Then he focused back on her. "Don't fight me on this, woman. You need a strong man right now, and I'm the one to be it."

And with that, he gestured with his free hand out of the pavilion. His other arm was wrapped around her waist, but a simple spin would have her away from him and back to the dancers. And if she did such a thing, he would let her go. A man could knock his brains against a stone wall for only so long.

But to his shock and pleasure, she nodded meekly and took a step in the direction he bid. He was quick to keep her beside him, pressed to his hip as they crossed onto the grass and then deeper into the pleasure garden.

He walked quickly, moving them away from the various expressions of the *ton*. He had no interest in what they thought and had no wish to clutter Mairi's mind with them either. Which meant it was the Dark Path for them.

He was still pondering what he would say to her when she broke the silence between them.

"You are right. I've no cause to be angry at my father for finding a wife. He's been alone for so long. I'm pleased that he found someone to warm his bed."

She sounded anything but pleased, and so he tucked her tighter still against his side.

"He hasn't been alone," Connall reminded her. "You've been with him, and no father could love a daughter more. Whatever he feels for Miss Allen will not change what is between the two of you."

She jolted in his arms, twisting slightly to look at him. "And is that why you think I'm hurting? Because I want my father's love for myself alone?"

He slowed his steps, staying beneath the glow of a lantern long enough to study her face in detail. She seemed both outraged and amused. "It's only natural," he said slowly. "You've been the sole woman—"

"I'm not that selfish to deny my father such a thing. I just thought..." She grimaced. "He and my mother were a love for all time. That's what he told me every night as I went to bed. That I was born of their love and that nothing could be so perfect or so pure."

"That's not changed."

"Hasn't it? He's grieved my mother for my whole life. He's told me of the day they first met, the color of her hair and the sound of her laugh. When deep in his cups, he talked about how she fit in his arms and that there could never be another. And he's lived mired in that grief for my whole life. I thought him a broken man."

"I know it," Connall said. He'd spent some of those drunken nights with her father listening to the tale of that great love. He'd even fancied that he and Mairi could have such a thing as well.

"And now he's better?" Mairi asked. "Now the love that cut him for a quarter of a century...is healed?" She pressed her hands to her temple. "I cannot conceive it."

Connall frowned, feeling completely at sea. "That's not a bad thing, is it? That a new woman has eased his loneliness?"

"Of course, it's a good thing! I want him happy!" She was all but shouting, and he could not reconcile the pain in her tone with what she actually said.

"Damn it, woman. Make sense!"

"I can't!" she cried back, clearly miserable.

He took a moment to study her. She stood there with her head bowed and her shoulders compressed against her neck. She looked like a person tensed for a blow. He might not understand the things that drove her, but he knew what she needed. So he enfolded her in his arms, wrapped her in his protection, and used his own body to keep her safe until she sorted through whatever it was that gripped her.

He didn't say a word. He didn't need to. She fell against him and cried silently. Tears wet his tartan and his chest while he held her tight.

In time, the storm passed. She cleaned her face and pulled back. And when she spoke, he held her tenderly as the knot of pain in his own chest eased.

"I have lived all my life with his grief, Connall. I watched true love tear him apart." She looked up at him. "That is all I knew of love," she said. "The devastating grief when it ends."

She stared at him a long time. There was a message there for him, but he didn't dare guess at it. She had to come to the statement herself, and so he held silent.

"How can such pain be healed so quickly? I've only been gone a few weeks."

"It's been twenty-five years, Mairi. How long did you want him to grieve?"

She shook her head. "I didn't want him to grieve," she huffed. "It's just…"

"It's what you thought love was? Decades of loneliness and pain—"

"When it's gone. Yes."

He was beginning to understand. "And now you wonder if it were a true love?"

"It was," she said firmly, as if trying to convince herself.

"Aye," he agreed. "There have been willing lasses aplenty for your father. I've seen them make advances to him. You have, too."

"I have."

"He didn't take up with a single one—"

"Not until now. Until Miss English Bluestocking Teacher."

He chuckled at her description of Miss Allen. Then he pressed a kiss to her forehead and turned them away from the light. This was a conversation to be had in shadows as they walked apart from gossipy ears.

"She must be very special woman, mustn't she?" he offered.

Mairi shrugged. "Maybe." Then she huffed out a breath. "I thought her a very nice woman when we met. Independent and smart."

He smiled. "Sounds like someone else I know."

"Who?"

He snorted. "You, you bloody fool. She's as fiercely herself as you are, or so Finn said." He pulled her tight. "Can you not wish them happy?"

"Of course, I can. I do! It just surprised me, is all."

And now came the sticking part. He tugged her into the shadows as he turned her to face him. "And what does this mean about us, Mairi? What does it make you think about our love?" He felt her stiffen beneath him, but he would not let her run from this now. "I know you love me, Mairi MacAdaidh. You have since we were children running wild through the moors."

She frowned at him, shoving him back with a pointed finger. Or she tried. This time, he refused to budge no matter how hard she poked. "A child's love and a woman's are different things."

"Aye." He cupped her cheek. "And I've a man's love for you. Will you not admit what you feel for me?"

He felt the tension in her body ratchet up a notch further. Her shoulders felt like stone, her mouth pursed, and her brows drew down as if in preparation for a blow. When she spoke, the words sounded forced through a constricted throat.

"You know how hard life is, Connall Aberbeag. Do you know the funerals I attend? It's not just the old who perish from sickness. My own mother died before she saw thirty."

"Aye." As chatelaine for the MacCleal, she would have seen every illness, every infected wound, every soul taken before his time.

"Should I doom you to such a life of grief? Or myself with all the chances you take?"

He shook his head. "It's been a long time since I was reckless. And I only did it then to catch your attention."

"And well you did," she snapped. "Every time you leaped across a ravine, every time you swam a rushing river, I thought of your body crushed and broken. And of my father's grief at being left alive when his love had gone."

Her words shocked him. He thought she cared nothing for him when in truth, she had been worried for him? And afraid of life without him? A clever man would say something now to ease her fears. A smart man would be able to logic her out of the risk. But he had no words to offer her. Life was uncertain. Death came for the quick as well as the slow. And yet, he would not lose her to fear. That he would not abide.

So he kissed her. There in the shadows or standing at an altar before God, he would not hide his love for her. Nor would he let her run from hers for him.

He did not hold back as he took her mouth. He slanted his lips over hers, reveling in her mew of surrender. How he loved her soft gasp accompanied by a sound of need. He knew it well after their night together. And he claimed it now with a thrust of his tongue.

God, how he wanted this woman. She was everything to him, and he'd be damned if he let her go. He told her that with his touch and his tongue. He took her mouth, he caressed her bottom, and he pulled her tight against him, so she could feel the length and heat of his need for her.

And when he had breath, he whispered in her ear. "I will no' give this up out of fear, Mairi MacAdaidh."

He thought to feel her melt then. She had already half surrendered to him by allowing his kiss, his touch, and his heat. Instead, something different happened.

She stiffened in shock. The change was instant and distressing. Her body went rigid, and she shoved backwards from him. His instinct was to grip her tight, but he would not hold her against her will. Still, his eyes shot open and he—

He heard a hard voice in his ear.

"Move one inch, gov, and I'll gut you, then have her."

Chapter Twenty-Five

MAIRI FELT THE slide of a blade cut across her ribs, sharp with pain. She knew the feel of a knife as it cut through her clothing and her flesh, but still the shock of it—coming during her moment with Connall—left her reeling and confused. Then rough hands grabbed her shoulders and hauled her back. She clutched onto Connall—of course, she did—but with blood seeping down her side and the hard grip of cruel hands, she had no strength to fight and no room to maneuver. Even a deep breath would make her wound worse.

She took one anyway. A scream was a woman's first defense.

A fist caught her in the throat before she could release it. Instead of calling for help, she ended up gagging as she dropped to her knees. Her dress stuck to her side, clammy with blood, and she heard Connall's choked-off roar of fury.

So he was caught, too.

It was dark here in this corner of the pleasure garden, but even choking as her throat throbbed with pain, she could look about her. Four men with knives stood around them while a fifth—the one who had punched her—smoothed his hand over her back and bum, squeezing her in a revolting manner.

"Not to my tastes," the man said, "but I'll take her anyway if I must."

She couldn't see the bastard, but she recognized his voice. It was that idiot Mr. Barrett. Why the hell wasn't he halfway across the Continent?

Still choking—she exaggerated her debilitation to hide her strength—she twisted enough to see Connall. He was held back by two thick-armed brutes. One had a knife to his throat, another pressed steel against his belly. She knew enough about knife play to know that either one could kill him, though the stomach wound would take longer.

"Touch her and I'll gut you," Connall rasped, rage twisting his features.

"Don't want to touch her," Mr. Barrett said. He slapped her bottom hard before stepping away from her with a mew of disgust. "So don't force me to."

"What do you want?" Connall said, his voice growing stronger.

"Keep it quiet," Mr. Barrett growled. "I've nothing to lose by killing you now." The words were spoken quietly, but there was an odd cadence to his words. She read desperation in the tone. And perhaps madness.

"You won't do it," Connall said, his voice only marginally lower. "You want something. What is it?"

Mr. Barrett stepped up to Connall, clearly trying to intimidate. But he hadn't the height or the presence to do that, but he still had the upper hand with two knives pressed to Connall's body.

"Get the women to confess," he said. "They stabbed Eugene. I'd nothing to do with it."

Connall sneered. "An' why would they do that?"

"Because if they don't, I'll do to them what I'm going to do to her." He paused as he rocked back on his heels. "I might do it to them anyway," he drawled. "Lucky for them, they didn't come down this way." He abruptly squatted down beside her. "So I got you."

Mairi shuddered at the hatred that burned in the man's gaze. It was so dark, so furious, that she doubted reason could touch the man. And yet, Connall tried.

"I'll talk to them," he said. "Let us go and I'll—"

Barrett surged to his feet. "Lie? Tell the constable and the court ridiculous things? I didn't kill Gene. I couldn't. I'm not a man who uses violence."

So he was insane. He stood there with a knife in his hand while he threatened horrible things, and still claimed he wasn't a violent man? Connall must have seen it too. She heard the placating tone in his voice as he tried to reach Barrett.

"They won't lie," he said. "I'll see to it. They'll tell the truth about everything. Just let us go so I can tell them."

"I don't believe you."

Neither did Mairi.

"They'll have to see, they'll have to *know* what will happen to them if they don't do as I say." He gestured to her. "So I'll do it to her."

Mairi couldn't believe the stupidity of the man. Did he truly think that Connall would allow such a thing? He could be restrained for only so long. The moment he had his chance, he would gut the Sassenach idiot. It was Mairi's job to see that he got that chance. Fortunately, she already had a wound that was bleeding enough to prove self-defense in a court of law.

She began to gag.

She wasn't the actress that some of the castle children were. She didn't know how to gag realistically enough that even the witch woman wondered if one were dying. But if she added in enough pretend hysteria, the men didn't know if she were dying, possessed of a spirit, or about to gut them with their own knives.

She planned for it to be that last one.

She wanted to attack Mr. Barrett. She bloody well hated the bastard now, but he was too far away. So when the nearest henchman hunched over her to see if she was dying, she surged upward straight into his face. Her forehead connected with his nose, and she heard the crunch of bone. He screamed and she added to it by punching him in the gut. But hell, he had a lot of gut. Her fist sunk in and lost power long before she hit his ribs.

Which meant she had little strength left to grab his knife arm and twist it aside. She did it anyway, her side screaming as she fought as she'd been trained.

The man didn't expect it, that was for sure, and she fought like a demon possessed, praying all the time that Connall was taking care of the others. She could handle one. That left four others for him.

She won in the end, slamming her elbow into the bastard's throat. He went down choking just as she had, leaving her free to grab his knife as he went down. Then she spun around, looking for Connall and any enemy she could gut.

What she saw instead was a knife going deep, straight into Connall's chest.

"No!" she screamed, seeing shock and dismay on Connall's face. Three men lay beaten at his feet, but the fourth had gotten through and killed Connall.

Mairi surged forward, screeching like a banshee. She jumped on the bastard who had gutted her love. She stabbed down with all her might even as she jerked his head back. The bastard was wiggly, that's for damn sure. She missed with her blade, but she got his head whipped around.

She clung to his back, screaming the whole time. Her knife was knocked away, but she was on the man's back. She would not let him go near Connall. She would kill him with her bare hands. But damnation, he was twisting beneath her, teetering and clawing at her.

Then he got his balance under him. With more power than she expected, he spun around, and she was thrown off. There was only so much she could do with her side slick with blood. His hair was greasy and slid out of her grasp. Damn, damn, damn!

She flew backwards with a thump that jarred all the way up her spine.

Thankfully, all the screaming had done its work. Even while she was falling through the air, she realized others were running forward. Others were exclaiming in horror or crying out for help.

They would see that the bastard didn't escape. Or they'd be stupid gawkers. Either way, the attack was over. All she cared about was Connall. He would not spill his lifeblood now. Not here. Not before she said all she had to say to him.

"Connall!" she cried as soon as she had breath. Then she scrambled up onto all fours as she righted herself. "Connall, you bloody bastard, you'll not die on me. Not before I say what I've got to say. Connall!"

She looked on the ground for his bleeding body. She twisted this way and that, seeing the unconscious henchmen scattered about. And then she finally, blessedly, found him, standing over Mr. Barrett with his fists clenched and a murderous look in his eyes.

He was alive!

She was just about to call out when she saw Mr. Barrett twist around on the ground. He had a pistol in his hand which he tried to aim straight at Connall's heart. A pistol held in a steady hand that could not fail to miss.

"No!" It was all she could get out, but she needn't have bothered.

Connall had seen the pistol and kicked hard at it. He missed the gun, but hit the hand that held it. And his motion continued on to slam into the bastard's head.

Mairi heard a crunch of bone. There wasn't even a gasp as the man tumbled backwards. Then she heard the gurgle. Not the death rattle. Not quite yet. But she knew the sounds of death and knew that Mr. Barrett would not live long enough to trouble them again.

She fell backwards onto her heels, her breath sawing in and out as her side burned from her wound. But all she saw was Connall as he dropped down before her and wrapped her in his arms.

"Mairi, love. Mairi," he murmured as he pressed her to him. But a moment later, he pulled back, his hand slick with blood.

"He stabbed you," she said, her voice tight with hysteria. "I saw it!"

She ran her hand across his chest, feeling for his wound. It had been fast. Battles always were. She'd been fighting herself, but she knew what she'd seen. The knife had plunged into his chest. She'd seen it...she'd seen...

"He missed me, Mairi."

"No, I saw it—"

"I twisted. I caught the blade in my plaid."

His voice was tight with fear or pain. She didn't know what. He was hurt. She'd seen it. She searched his eyes. He looked pale.

"Mairi, you need to tell me what hurts."

What? "I saw you stabbed."

"No, love. I'm fine. You're the one hurt."

She was? She didn't feel it.

He lifted her up, holding her close. "I'm going to take you home now," he said.

"Stop! You'll hurt your wound."

"Hush, love. I've got you safe."

"But—"

"I've got ye." Then he carried her away.

CHAPTER TWENTY-SIX

WHEN CONNALL SAID he was taking her home, Mairi thought he meant to the countess's London home. It wasn't until after the doctor bandaged her wound that she realized he meant Scotland. That the maid was to pack her clothing as soon as she was well enough. Then they both would return to where they belonged.

That's what he said. "She's coming with me to where we both belong."

And that, of course, was Scotland. To his castle, to his people, to a place where she would become mistress. Where he would stand by her side and she by his until some tragedy struck one of them down.

Strangely enough, the horror of that thought hit her differently now than before. Because all through the doctor's visit and while she gave her statement to the constable, she kept replaying the moment she'd seen Connall stabbed through the heart. She saw it in her mind's eye, she relived the searing pain of it, and she knew without a shadow of a doubt that to live such a moment again would kill her.

It would destroy her heart, tear her sanity apart, and leave her broken in its wake.

And the only way to ease the pain was to hold onto his strong hand, to touch his healthy body, and to hear the rumble of his voice so powerful against her ear.

Somehow, he understood. Or maybe he needed to be as close to her as she was to him because she felt his hand constantly seeking out hers. He stood near enough for her to always see him, if not actually touch. And when the doctor had to inspect the long slash of her wound, he remained in the room a glowering, angry, protective, wonderful presence as the doctor declared it not so deep as to be mortal, but definitely requiring rest and proper care.

Fortunately, Mairi already knew that. She'd given the recipe for the unguent to the butler. It took an hour to get it made. An hour required for Connall to be assured that she would not perish. For him to send the doctor away and push out the women who hovered in anxious fear. And when the butler finally brought it up to her, it was he who insisted that he tend her.

She allowed it because she wanted it as much as he did. She lay still in the now quiet room while he gently dabbed salve into her wound. And while he did, she replayed the moment he'd been stabbed over and over in her thoughts. She'd seen it, and yet, here he was as hale as ever. In fact, he was the one tending to her wound.

The conflicting thought had her catching his hand and drawing his attention to her face.

"Does it hurt?" he asked. "Are you in pain?"

How to answer that? "I have been an idiot," she said.

His eyes widened as a broad grin cut through his expression. "Mairi, my love, it happens so rarely that you are unaccustomed to it. I am glad you finally recognize the situation."

She glowered at him. "I am being serious."

"As am I." She would believe him if not for the twinkle in his eye. Then he brought her hand to his mouth. "Please tell me what you mean."

"I thought if I never loved you, it would not hurt so much when you died."

His brows rose. "And have you been waiting for me to die?"

Constantly. "You took risks as a boy—"

"I was a boy."

"And you have been a starred man ever since. Everything you touch turns to gold. You win every contest, meet every challenge, manage your clan to profit. Always."

He shook his head. "You know how hard I work. It is not luck or the stars."

She knew. She also knew that misfortune comes to every soul. "I did not want to love you when your luck turns."

His expression sobered. "Did you think you could control that? That you can choose who you love and who you do not?"

Of course, she did. Of course, she had. But denying love was not the same thing as not being in love. "I saw the knife kill you. I saw your death," she said, her voice breaking.

"I am not dead. I am right here." He pressed her hand to his chest. "See? My heart beats."

"I would not live broken like my father. I would not love you when I might lose you." Her hand was flat on his chest, and she felt his heart beat strong and solid beneath it. "I was an idiot."

"You were afraid, but I will not let you live like that anymore. I need you too much."

He needed her? She needed him. "I cannot live without you a second longer. I love you, Connall. If I am to lose you, then I will love you now because I cannot stop it anyway."

He pressed her hand to his mouth, and she felt the tremble of his lips against hers. Then he pulled her fingers away and spoke in a strained voice. "I saw the knife cut you. I felt your blood on my hands."

"Not a deep cut."

"You did not stand up. You were choking as if you could not breathe."

"Pretense. So I could fight when it was time."

He nodded. "I know. And yet, I saw it, too. I saw your death."

"I am fine."

"I will not wait any longer, Mairi. Be my wife. For as long as God gives us, be with me."

Exactly the words she'd wanted to hear. "Yes," she said. "Yes, yes, yes."

He met her mouth to mouth, heart to heart. He was careful with her wound, but she wasn't. She clutched her to him and opened herself to all the love she'd denied for so long. She loved him. No matter what came next, she would see it through with him until the end.

And the moment her heart opened, he poured all his love in.

They kissed with all that love swirling between them. They held onto one another as if each was the most precious gift ever. And when she looked into his eyes, she knew she had found what she'd been searching for.

"Will you marry me?" he asked, his voice low.

"Yes. I've said—"

"Tonight. In the Scottish way. If your wound doesn't pain you?"

No wound could hurt her so much that she would deny him. She grinned. "I will marry you in every way."

A promise, but it was as good as a vow before a priest. And so they looked at each other, suspended in time as they absorbed what they'd both just said. One second or one century, she had no idea how much time passed until the countess knocked on the door.

They came back to themselves with a jolt, then turned as one when she entered. She was slow as she opened the door, and her expression was hopeful.

"We are wed now," they said together. They were not in Scotland where a simple statement of marriage would make it legal, but in this room, it would serve. They would have a ceremony at home with their family all around. But for now, this was enough.

The countess clapped her hands together in delight. "Well, it's about time. And poor Mr. Weissman will have to look elsewhere."

Mairi frowned, suspicion slipping into her thoughts. "Was

there ever a Mr. Weissman? Or did you make him up?"

"Of course, there are several Mr. Weissmans," the lady said with mock outrage. "And I'm sure I could have found one of them to offer for you." She winked at them. "But I am glad that I am no longer put to the effort." Then she waved at Connall. "Now come out of there. We can announce your engagement—"

"Wedding."

She waved the technicality aside. "At tonight's ball."

Connall shook his head. "You will have to do it without me."

"Yes, yes, I know. But first, you must tell the others."

Iseabail and Sadie abruptly pushed their way inside. "We heard. We think it's about time. And we love you both!"

Kisses were shared all around. Everyone asked about her wound and her health. Everyone clapped Connall on the back and told him he had won the greatest of all prizes in her. He did not deny it, and everyone made merry until Mairi yawned.

It was well after midnight now, and suddenly all were much too exhausted to stay awake. They gave her a kiss on the cheek and wished her happy. Not a word was said about Connall retiring to his room, and he made no indication that he would leave. It was all very scandalous from the English point of view, but the Scots knew a deed done even when it had yet to occur.

When at last Connall shut the door behind them, he turned to Mairi. "Love, I can wait—"

"Come to me, please," she said. "I will not sleep one wink without you beside me."

His smile was rueful. "If I cannot hold you tonight, I will have nightmares for sure. Mairi, I was so afraid."

She pulled him to her. The memory of the knife plunging into him came back to her, inescapable no matter how much she tried to push it aside. Only his hand in hers helped it fade.

"Take off the plaid, my lord," she said.

"Do you need help with your nightrail?" he asked.

They helped each other as if they were unwrapping their future. She was eager, tugging at the fabric of his tartan, shocked when she saw where it had been cut, but able to move beyond the slash to the naked man beneath. He pulled at her clothing carefully, being gentle with her body even as he eased her out of the fabric. Then he lifted her into his arms as he slid into bed beside her.

Such strength he had, such power as he lay beside her.

"I know of no other woman who could be cut as you and still come out fighting."

"I thought they'd killed you. Of course, I fought."

"I thought you hurt such that I could not save you. I wanted to rend them limb from limb."

She felt the shudder that went through his body and knew its echo trembled inside her. She kissed him not to end the fear but to weather it together. He rode it out with her, deepening the kiss because he always made things deeper, stronger, and so much better.

They took their time touching each other. His expression darkened whenever he touched her bandage, so she pulled his hand upward to cup her breast. He teased her nipple while she gasped at the pleasure he stroked through her. And when he bent his head to suckle there, she envisioned their child. A babe born of their love would be a miracle. No matter if she lost him the next day, the child would be a gift from God and from him. One that would keep him alive even if the unthinkable happened.

That was what her father felt, she realized, whenever he looked at her with his eyes misty with tears. It wasn't grief, it was gratitude and love.

She wanted that now with a strength that startled her. So without double-guessing the feeling or doubting the truth of it, she surged upward. If it bothered her wound, she didn't feel it. All she wanted was Connall inside her, creating his babe in her womb.

He gasped when she pushed him onto his back, but he grinned when she straddled him. He held her steady as she settled on her knees while his cock teased unerringly close.

"You always surprise me, Mairi," he said with a grin.

"Did you think I would wait when I finally know what I want?"

"Ach, no. I'm just grateful you came to your senses."

She laughed at his confidence and then she tilted her hips. "Make me your wife, Connall Aberbeag, for I will have no other."

"With pleasure," he said as he thrust into her.

She cried out in shock, not at the penetration, but at the pleasure. She had heard of a maiden's pain since a very young age. But this wasn't pain, this was connection. A bond that couldn't be broken. A man who took her as his own.

Pure joy as he filled her.

Pure pleasure as he moved inside her.

She set the rhythm, and he matched it.

As she took control, he pleasured her breasts.

As his breath became ragged, he slipped his thumb between her folds.

Fire shot through her body as he worked her.

Wildness took hold as she alternately opened to him then squeezed him tight.

Her body spoke the words, *Love me.*

His answered, *Forever.*

And together they soared.

And maybe they went high enough in heaven to catch a child.

CHAPTER TWENTY-SEVEN

ISEABAIL HAD NEVER seen a couple happier to travel hundreds of miles together in a closed carriage. Mairi and Connall left as soon as the doctor declared her wound did not bear an infection. No doubt there were women throughout the *ton* who grieved the loss of an eligible duke, but no one at the countess's home was surprised by the bliss on the two newlywed's faces.

The couple pulled away in their carriage at dawn and though there were hugs and kisses from all around, the two still managed to leave while bickering about a one-hundred pound dowry Mairi thought she was owed. Connall and Mairi would always bicker, it seemed, even in the midst of blissful union.

A minute after their carriage pulled away, the countess declared it too early for decent people to be awake. She went straight back to her bed. Sadie laughed as she too disappeared upstairs to claim Mairi's abandoned room as her own. That left Iseabail to make the slow climb to the bedroom that was now hers alone.

She didn't rush. With Connall gone, too much fear gripped her to make her move quickly anywhere. She knew it was ridiculous. Her uncle was still in Scotland, hopefully none the wiser as to her whereabouts. But he was a canny old man and her disappearance had no doubt infuriated him. No soul, and especially not a girl's, could escape his iron grip. Or so she'd been told—and shown—from the moment her parents had died, and he'd had care of her.

Even weeks after her escape to London, she'd seen his men in every shadow. She jumped at the sound of rough male voices. She cringed at every quick movement. And the idea that Connall and Mairi had been attacked in Vauxhall left her in a cold sweat of panic.

Thankfully, almost no one knew her true identity. The necklace that proclaimed her heritage was gone, stolen by a highwayman. And though she'd grieved it at the time, now she found it to be a blessing. If she found a husband and changed her name, there was no one to connect her to her uncle's clan.

That was good. The land of her birth held nothing but pain for her. And yet, she feared that somewhere, somehow, her past would seize her in a very literal sense. Until the day she wed, her uncle could grab her and force her to marry his kin. She would be trapped forever in that horrible place with no hope left to her.

That thought kept her awake every night. It was the shadow that haunted her days.

So it was that when she entered her bedroom and a man stepped out from behind the curtain, she was quick to dash to the dresser and the dirk she kept there. She whipped around, knife raised while she filled her lungs with a scream that would wake the entire neighborhood.

"I wouldn't do that, lass," said a voice she remembered, "else how can we negotiate?"

Her scream froze in her throat, not held out of terror, but suspended as her mind caught up with her senses.

A huge man leaned against the corner post of her bed, a cheeky grin on his rugged face. He wasn't handsome, per se, but he had a brutal kind of charm built of strength and hard living. He looked like a Scotsman to her, if such a man could have good cheer and a wicked smile that didn't frighten her. Her breath eased out of her chest, the scream gone.

"I remember you," she said as she looked at his dark clothing. It was not the attire of an aristocrat, but it was all exquisitely made of the finest materials. A rich rogue, then, dressed as a highwayman might. "Reuben Bates. The man who saved us from the highwaymen."

"The very same," he said as he swept off his hat and executed a courtly bow. "And you are the honorable Miss Iseabail Spalding, ward of Baron Bain. You're the granddaughter of the Earl of Spalding, and the only child of his daughter, Lady Alice." His grin widened. "You're also dowered with five-hundred gold pieces in a chest brought from the farthest corner of the earth."

She shook her head. "The dowry is long gone. The contents merely rumor."

"Oh no," he said with a cheeky grin. "It's real and a great deal more than a meager five-hundred pounds."

She blinked. "That's not possible."

"But it is." Then he fished into his pocket and pulled out her necklace. It flashed in the light, a dragon with a fat belly all done in the vague shape of a shield. "A pretty bauble this," he said as he turned it over in his hand. "Especially if one knows to do this." With the tip of his thumb, he twisted the hidden latch. The gold popped open and exposed a polished dark red stone, the dragon's heart.

Oh damn. Oh hell. Bad enough that he had the necklace of the honorable Miss Spalding. But that stone, one that when held up to the light revealed the six points of a star ruby, that told some people a great deal more about her parentage.

Panic rolled dark and cold down her spine, but she stuffed it down under a false air of casual surprise. "Oh, you found the catch," she said lightly. "It's not a very pretty stone underneath. I think that's why it was covered."

"That's not why," he said, humor lacing his tone. "Tell me about your mother, Miss Spalding. Tell me about what this stone meant to her."

He knew. Damnation, he knew the stories about her mother. Whispers that could be true or could be ridiculous tales told to frighten children. Even she didn't know.

"I don't know what you think you've heard," she began.

"But none of it's true?" he finished for her. "I think a little bit of it is true. And maybe a great deal more." His eyes seemed to twinkle. Was it greed? Lust? Humor? She didn't know and she couldn't look away.

"It's all exaggeration, rumor, and guesses."

He pushed off the bedpost to saunter forward. He was a big man, and he moved with the athletic ease of a warrior. Every movement was controlled, every step done lightly such that he could jump in any direction, counter every attack, and catch any prey.

She shied backwards, nervous even as he mesmerized her. "What do you want?"

He grinned as if she had just asked the question he'd been waiting for. "What I want is more than you can imagine. What I want from you is something we must discuss."

She held up her hands as if to push him back. "We have nothing to discuss." Indeed, she wasn't even sure she wanted her necklace back. It came with a host of problems. And yet it was all she had of her mother.

"Nothing?" he taunted, his expression dark. "I think we do."

She swallowed, painfully aware that she now had another enemy, one who seemed more dangerous even than her uncle.

"Tell me, Miss Spalding, what you would give to have this trinket back?" He held her necklace out between them.

"I have my pin money," she said. "It's not much—" She cut off her words when he touched her cheek, trailing his finger down along her jaw. Sensation burned in its wake as he tilted her face to look up at him.

"And what would you give to keep your secrets hidden away? How many people know the full truth about your mother?"

No one. Not even her. But several people suspected things, her uncle knew a bit more, and she... Well, she was trapped between her mother's past and her own fanciful dreams. And all of it was deadly to her in the wrong hands or if twisted the wrong way.

She couldn't let this continue. It didn't matter if he terrified her, she had to break his spell on her.

So she lifted her chin and faced down this rough man though it took everything in her not to tremble in fear. "You imagine things," she said. "It's nothing but a—"

"A witch's talisman. A sorcerer's amulet. *A cursing stone.*"

"It is no such thing!" she exploded, though she knew her uncle thought it to be just that. She tried to grab it from the blackguard's hand, but he was too quick for her. He jerked it away while still holding it tantalizingly close between them.

"Some call it that." His brows arched as he looked at her. "And some would call you a great deal worse for having it."

"Keep it then," she snapped. It had only caused her grief.

"I might," he returned. "Indeed, I have a mind to study the thing further. But in the meantime, what could you pay me, Miss Spalding, to stop me from telling everyone in London about your mother's witchcraft?"

What could she say? Even the whisper of such a thing could kill a woman. The Witchcraft Act had been repealed nearly a century ago, but men still hunted for them no matter what the crown declared. The information that her mother was not only a witch, but the most renowned witch in a hundred years would lead men to hunt Iseabail down. Death would be the smallest of horrors they would do to her.

"It's not true," she whispered. "She was just a woman."

"The truth doesn't matter," he returned. "It never has."

He was right about that. If her mother had possessed any magic at all, Iseabail's father would still be alive. Her uncle would be in a grave somewhere, and Iseabail's life would be vastly different than it was now.

"You cannot tell anyone about this. The rumors alone could get me killed."

His thumb trailed across her lips, leaving a hot tingle in its wake. "Offer me something, Miss Spalding, but choose it well."

"I don't have anything," she cried.

"That's unfortunate because my silence is very, very expensive."

"What do you want?" she whispered. She had no choice. No one could know. "I'll give you anything."

He chuckled and the sound made her body shiver. "Imagine that," he drawled. "*Anything* is exactly what I want."

About the Author

A *USA Today* Bestseller, JADE LEE has been scripting love stories since she first picked up a set of paper dolls. Ball gowns and rakish lords caught her attention early (thank you Georgette Heyer), and her fascination with historical romance began. Author of more than 30 regency romances, Jade has a gift for creating a lively world, witty dialogue, and hot, sexy humor. Jade also writes contemporary and paranormal romance as Kathy Lyons. Together, they've won several industry awards, including the *Prism—Best of the Best, Romantic Times Reviewer's Choice,* and *Fresh Fiction's* Steamiest Read. Even though Kathy (and Jade) have written over 60 romance novels, she's just getting started. Check out her latest news at www.KathyLyons.com, Facebook: JadeLeeAuthor, and Twitter: JadeLeeAuthor. Instagram: KathyLyonsAuthor.

Lightning Source UK Ltd.
Milton Keynes UK
UKHW020704110422
401395UK00008B/182